BOBBY

BASEBALL

ALSO BY
Robert Kimmel Smith
CHOCOLATE FEVER

JELLY BELLY

THE WAR WITH GRANDPA

MOSTLY MICHAEL

Robert Kimmel Smith

ILLUSTRATED BY

Alan Tiegreen

Delacorte Press

Published by
Delacorte Press
Bantam Doubleday Dell Publishing Group, Inc.
666 Fifth Avenue
New York, New York 10103

Library of Congress Cataloging in Publication Data
Smith, Robert Kimmel [date of birth]
    Bobby Baseball / by Robert Kimmel Smith :
    illustrated by Alan Tiegreen.
        p.   cm.
    Summary: Ten-year-old Bobby is passionate about baseball and
convinced that he is a great player. The only problem is to get
a chance to prove his skill, especially to his father.
    ISBN 0-385-29807-2
    [1. Baseball—Fiction. 2. Self-perception—Fiction.
3. Fathers and sons—Fiction.] I. Tiegreen, Alan, ill.
II. Title.
PZ7.S65762Bo   1989
[Fic]—dc19   89-1175
                                                           CIP
                                                            AC

Book design by Andrew Roberts

Manufactured in the United States of America

October 1989

10   9   8   7   6   5   4   3

BG

For the Dodgers I loved,
the *Brooklyn* Dodgers,
and for Red Barber

CONTENTS

Contents

1

About Me

I may as well start by writing down my name. But not all of it.

My name is Robert E. Ellis. The E. is for Ebenezer, a grandpa of mine who died before I was born. I think Ebenezer is a horrible name, even for a person who is dead.

I never tell anybody my middle name. Because I know there are some wise guys in the world who would give me a nickname I really hate. My big brother, Sammy, who knows my middle name, teases me sometimes by calling me Sneezer.

I think a person should decide his own nickname for himself. My friend Jason calls me Bobby. Kids I know in school call me Bob or Bobby, or even Robby. My folks call me Bobby, but once in a while my dad will call me Bob-o. All those names are okay with me, and definitely better than Sneezer.

1

But I have already decided my baseball nickname, which every big league player has to have.

I am going to be known as Bobby "Baseball" Ellis.

This is a great nickname and one that is sure to be remembered. Sometimes I say it to myself under my breath and I really like the sound of it.

I know "Bobby Baseball" sounds a little show-offy. The truth is I do act like a show-off sometimes. I can also behave like a stupid jerk and a real nerdo with no trouble at all.

I am nowhere near being a perfect person.

My biggest problem is my terrible temper. When it grabs me, I can go bananas in two seconds. I try to hold it back, I really do, but mostly I can't. Once, when I was four years old, I bit Sammy's hand so bad he still has a red raggedy scar near his thumb.

Trouble is, when my temper takes over I still act like I'm four years old.

The biggest thing in my life is baseball. Dad says I have baseball in my blood. I know he's right. I think about baseball a lot. Like most of the time. I also dream about baseball. Even when I am awake.

I've gotten into trouble more than once by dreaming about baseball. Mostly in school and mainly in math class. Math and me don't get along too well. I figure that's because my head is round and math is very square and logical. So all that square math just bounces off my round head and never gets in there.

The only class in school I like is language arts, especially creative writing. I can write baseball stories for a week straight and never run out of ideas. Miss DeBoer, my teacher, is getting sick of it. "Another baseball story?" she said when I handed in the last one. "Robert, there are other things in life besides baseball, you know."

I suppose Miss DeBoer is right. But my head is stuffed with batting averages and all-time records. I know most of the important stats by heart, and I keep memorizing more of them.

You see, I have been planning on becoming a major league pitcher since I was seven years old. Someday I will be up at Cooperstown making my speech when they put me in the Baseball Hall of Fame. I have not actually begun writing my speech yet. There is plenty of time for that. First I will have to get into the big leagues, which will take a while since I am only ten years old.

Once I am a big-leaguer I will begin writing my terrific baseball books. It's a smart thing to do in the off-season, when it's too cold to play ball. I'm surprised that more big-leaguers haven't done this. Maybe it's because few of them can write as good as me.

If that sounds show-offy, I can't help it. I really do think I was born to be a baseball immortal, and also a great writer.

2

About My Family

My dad's name is Charles "Chuck" Ellis, and I have his baseball card.

Dad played for three years in the St. Louis Cardinals' farm system when he was eighteen, nineteen, and twenty years old. The baseball card is from the Arkansas Travelers, Dad's last team. The picture on the front of the card shows him catching a toss at second base. The back of the card has his stats.

The best Dad hit was in his second year, .243. He hit two home runs that year, which is not a lot. He was a sure-handed second baseman, a good glove man, and his dream was to make the major leagues. He never did.

When I ask him about it, he always smiles and says the same thing: "Couldn't hit the curveball, Bobby, and that was all she wrote."

Also he had fallen in love with my mother by

then, Molly Herr, and he missed her a lot during those long summers when he played double-A ball in Little Rock. So he quit baseball and came back to town and married Mom. Then he began selling insurance, and that's what he still does.

Dad brought up Sammy and me to love baseball. From before I can remember, there was a shiny new baseball in my crib for me to play with. Dad says that when I was a baby, I used to put that baseball in my mouth and bite on it when I had a new tooth coming in.

I still have that same baseball, teeth marks and all. It's not new anymore, of course, but scuffed up and turning yellow. I always pick it up and toss it in my hand when I am up in my room working on my writing.

My mom teaches English in the high school in town. She believes that a person who does not read books is on the road to wasting his life. Mom taught me to read when I was four years old, but I didn't start to really love reading until I found my dad's collection of baseball books. It takes up a whole wall in the living room and it keeps growing.

Dad buys all the new baseball books and reads them, then Sammy grabs them, unless I beat him to it. Mostly the new ones are about star players and teams that won the World Series. A lot of them have bad language—the *F* curse and stuff like that—but I like them anyway.

What I really love to read and reread are the old books and stories. I like John R. Tunis, William Heyliger, Ralph Henry Barbour, and Dad's old *Saturday*

Evening Post magazines that have Ring Lardner stories in them.

Right now I am reading "The Southpaw" by Mark Harris. It's terrific, except for the lovey-dovey stuff that I skip right over. Sammy says I will understand it better when I am his age, which is fourteen.

Can you see why I am so sure I am going to become a Hall of Fame ballplayer and also a great writer?

I have been writing things in my Baseball Book for three years now. I call it my Baseball Book, even though it's only a ninety-eight-cent composition book with a hard cover and lined pages. I write facts, ideas, and thoughts about baseball in there. Also some stories I make up. Here is something I wrote last year.

●   ●   ●

An official major league baseball weighs between 5 and 5 1/4 ounces. It is made of a cork center with tightly wrapped yarn around that and a cover of horse hide.

It is also hard as a rock.

If baseball was played with something soft, like a tennis ball, then everyone including girls and old people could play it.

But the ball is hard and the game is too.

3

Hot-Stove League

The only good thing about snow in March is that if you get enough of it, they close the school.

Today we got thirteen inches, a blizzard, and we got to stay home. That's the good part. The bad part is that Sammy and me had to go outside and shovel all that snow.

We went out after breakfast, a late breakfast because Mom was home from school too. She didn't bother waking us when she heard on the radio about the schools closing. Dad was home as well, and Grandpa was still sleeping.

Sammy and me got dressed like Eskimos, grabbed the shovels from the basement, and slipped out the back door. It was cold out there, windy too, and the snow kept blowing in our faces. It was worse for Sammy because he wears these thick eyeglasses and the snow blew on them and made it hard for him to see.

We cleared the front walk first, the steps and the

porch next. Sammy kept stopping and wiping off his glasses. By then we weren't cold anymore. Shoveling snow warms you up in a hurry. I felt all sweaty under my shirt and sweater and lumberjacket, which is what Grandpa calls my plaid parka.

We took a break and huddled against the big oak tree on our front lawn, out of the wind. "There's a ball game on TV today," I said to Sammy.

"Great," said Sammy. He didn't sound like he meant it.

"Red Sox against the Pirates at one o'clock. They're playing down in Florida."

"You're nuts," Sammy said. "How can you even think about baseball when my teeth are chattering?"

"Baseball is my life," I said, trying to be funny. Sammy punched me on the arm, which is what I expected.

"Bobby Baseballhead," Sammy called me. "I think your pointy head is made out of yarn with a cork center."

"American or National League ball?" I asked.

"Neither. You're too small to be a regulation ball. You're probably one of those cheap baby baseballs where the cover comes off when you hit it."

We scrunched in close together against the tree and watched the wind and snow for a while. My breath came up in a white cloud and whirled away in the wind.

"Do you think Dad will let me be on his team?" I asked.

Sammy thought for a few seconds. "Yeah," he said, "probably."

I felt good hearing Sammy say that. This was the

year I graduated to Mustang League, where my dad always coaches the Hawks. Mustang wasn't like Learning League, which I had played in since I was seven. Now I was ten years old and I could begin playing real baseball, with real pitching and stealing bases, not just baby ball.

"Dad will say he probably shouldn't coach you," said Sammy, "like he told me. But in the end he will. If you insist on it."

"Then I will," I said.

"Right."

"Dad's really the best coach, isn't he?" I asked.

"He's great," Sammy said. "But there are other good coaches in the league. You could play on a different team."

"Why wouldn't I want to be on Dad's team?" I said. "I mean, he's my dad."

Sammy smiled in a funny way and wiped off his glasses. "You'll see, sucker," he said. "Just wait until you mess up and you'll find out your dad's a hardnose."

"I won't mess up," I said.

"Right," said Sammy. "You're Mister Perfect, who'll never make an error in his life. Get real, will you? Wait till you make a mental mistake, which you will, and Dad asks you if you're asleep out there. Or when he makes you run three laps around the field and your tongue'll be hanging out."

"So what?" I said. "I can take it."

"Oh, yeah? How about when Dad asks you to do something you don't want to do? And you have to do it because he's your dad and not just a coach. Then you'll find out maybe it would have been better to play ball for a stranger, not your dad."

On this cold day there was a lot of heat in Sammy's voice. But I really didn't understand it. I thought it would be the greatest thing in the world to have Dad as my coach. After all, Dad was the one who taught me everything about baseball.

It was Dad who threw me thousands of ground balls in the backyard until I learned how to catch them. It was Dad who bought me my first baseball glove, my first bat, and he even gave me a new glove last Christmas. And it was Dad who took me to the park, put me near the fence, and threw hours of batting practice to me until I got the hang of hitting a ball.

I think Sammy is nuts. Playing for Dad's team was all I wanted this year.

Sammy was really a terrific ballplayer, a catcher, until his eyes started to go bad. His eyeglasses kept getting thicker and thicker until he couldn't really see too far at all.

When you're a catcher and you can't see the ball, you'd better get out of there. Which is exactly what Sammy did. Now he just coaches Dad's team and helps out because he still loves the game so much.

"Let's go, Sneezer," Sammy said, getting up. "We may as well start clearing the sidewalk and that long driveway."

We picked up our shovels and worked about an hour, until there was a path for Mom's car and Dad's station wagon to get out to the street.

Sammy started walking toward the back door, when I grabbed his arm and stopped him. "Hey," I said, "how about you throw me some batting practice?"

"Throw you *what* ?"

"Some snowballs," I said. "I'll hit 'em with my shovel."

Sammy started laughing. "You're a crazy kid, you know that?"

"Come on," I said. "Just a few."

Sammy shook his head, but he began making a snowball, so I backed away and took up my stance. I had to choke up on the shovel a lot. But it was okay. I managed to hit quite a few, even though they busted apart when I smacked them.

"Fastballs now!" I yelled, and Sammy wound up and threw one at my head, which knocked me down in the snow. "Over the plate, sucker!" I yelled, laughing.

I hit a couple of good ones. Then we heard a rapping on the kitchen window. There was Dad, a grin on his face, waving at us to come back in the house.

Ball game called because of snow, and a father.

●　　●　　●

A baseball has 216 red stitches on it. I know because I counted them.

Dad says that major league baseballs are made in a country called Haiti. Ladies in a factory down there sew every ball by hand. They are the ones who put the 216 stitches on with red yarn.

I think that is really weird. Why don't they make American baseballs right here in America?

4

Off-Day

By the time Sammy and me put the shovels away and changed out of our sweaty clothes, Grandpa was in the kitchen.

Let me tell you about Grandpa. His name is Albert Herr and he's my mom's dad. Grandpa is pretty old, but he's still got a full head of black hair. His eyes are blue, like Mom's, and he's almost as tall as Dad. Grandpa is really in great shape. He walks miles when the weather is good, and he does a lot of sit-ups and push-ups every morning before breakfast. I once had a push-up contest with him and he did twenty-five. I was exhausted and flat on my stomach after ten.

Grandpa also reads a lot, almost as much as Mom. He likes Westerns, mainly, but if Mom recommends a book to him, he'll read it.

I sat down at the kitchen table next to Grandpa while Sammy made hot chocolate for himself and me.

13

Mom was sitting there too, in her chair at the end of the table, and she was reading a book. My mom is always reading one book or another, that being one of her main interests in life. Her favorite writer is a dead lady named Jane Austen, who wrote books a long time ago. Mom says that none of her books are about baseball. I once tried to read one of Jane Austen's books and I couldn't get past the first page. People must have talked funny in those olden days. They sure wrote funny.

"What's the fact for today?" Sammy asked Grandpa.

"Haven't found one yet," said Grandpa.

Grandpa reads just about every word in the newspaper every day. He likes to find funny little facts in the paper, the kind they stick on the bottom of the page to fill out a column.

"The fact of the day is that it's still snowing," said Sammy. He brought our hot chocolate to the table. "It may snow forever," he said. "The house may get buried in snow."

"Happened to a friend of mine lived up in Minnesota," said Grandpa. "The snow kept on snowing and just piled against his house up to the roof. Only the chimney stuck out. Spent the whole winter in the house, he did, and warm as toast. Didn't get to go outside until the snow melted in April."

"Grandpa," I said, "come on."

He looked at me real serious. "What?"

"Is this another one of your made-up stories?" I asked.

"What?" said Grandpa, looking like I'd just insulted him. "Do I make up stories?"

"You know you do," I said. That's the truth.
Grandpa does like to make up things and exaggerate,
mostly to be funny.

Dad came walking into the kitchen. "Nice job of
shoveling, you guys," he said. He poured himself a
cup of coffee. "If this snow ever decides to stop, I may
even get to the office."

Mom looked up from her book. "Surely you're not
thinking of going out in this mess?" she said.

"I'm thinking about it," said Dad.

"Chuck, stay home," she said.

"Okay," said Dad with a big smile, "you talked me
into it. I'll work on the telephone."

"We got a ball game on TV today," I said.

"More than one game," said Dad. "The Mets, the
Cubbies, and the Red Sox are all on cable."

"Let's watch all three," I said.

"Marooned in the snow with a family of baseball
nuts," said Mom. "How can you be interested in baseball when it's twenty degrees outside and snowing?"

Dad's eyes met mine and we both smiled.

"That's the best thing about it," Dad said. "Down
in spring training the sun'll be shining, it'll be seventy
degrees, and they'll be playing ball. It gives you hope
that summer is just around the corner."

"Summer?" said Mom. "It's still three weeks until
spring."

"Not in my heart," said Dad. "In my heart it's always summer."

For some reason that made Mom smile. Dad went
over to her and mussed her hair a little, then kissed her
on the neck. I could see Mom liked it, but I don't

know why. When Dad or Mom kisses me on the neck, it always makes me shiver.

"Fact of the day," Grandpa announced, looking up from his newspaper. "The largest lake in North America is Lake Superior, with an area of thirty-one thousand seven hundred square miles."

"That's superior, all right," said Dad. "What's the largest lake in the world, then?"

"Beats me," said Grandpa.

"The Caspian Sea," said Mom, not looking up from her book.

"How can it be a lake if it's a sea?" I asked.

"I don't know," said Mom. "Look it up in your encyclopedia." She always says that, and sometimes I even do.

After lunch, Sammy, Dad, and me settled down in the den, where the big color TV is. The Mets were playing the Orioles in Miami, and we watched that game for a few innings. But while the commercials were on, Dad switched to the Cubs–Padres game in Mesa, Arizona. It was great weather out in Arizona. Sunny and 74 degrees.

I love the way a big league ball field looks. It seems they have the greenest grass and the reddest dirt in the world. Dad says they put something in the dirt to make it red—brick dust. Whatever it is, I get this good feeling in my stomach when I look at a really pretty ball field. I just want to be out there on it, running around, catching a ground ball, sliding into second base.

The Padres had a man on first when their shortstop hit a single into right field. The Cubs' right fielder made a long throw on the fly all the way to third base.

But the Padres' runner was safe by a mile, and the batter ran down to second base behind him. "That's the way you lose ball games," said Dad. "Where should that throw have gone?"

"Second base," I said.

"Why?" asked Dad.

"To keep the batter from taking an extra base," I said.

"And to keep the double play in order," said Sammy.

"You got it," said Dad. "That should be an error on the right fielder, but you won't see it in the box score."

"A mental error," said Sammy.

"Right," said Dad. "You know why they call them mental errors? Because they make a manager lose his mind."

Sammy rolled his eyes at me, and I winked back at him. When we watched a ball game with Dad, he was always pointing out mental errors. He could forgive someone messing up a grounder or dropping a fly ball, but when a player didn't think . . . it drove Dad dippy.

That night, after I brushed my teeth and got into my pajamas, Dad came into my room to tuck me into bed. He really doesn't tuck me under the covers, the way he used to. He sits down on my bed for a minute, if he has time, and we talk.

"I'm thinking about the Hawks," I said to him. "I really want to play for you, Dad."

Dad made a face. "I don't know, Bob," he said, "in a lot of ways it's not a good idea."

"You're the best," I said.

Dad smiled at that. "There are other good

managers you could play for. Jack Sheridan, Whitey Pezzino, Jerry Wexler . . ."

"Why not you?"

"It can be a problem, Bob, for both of us. I'll have to be very careful not to show favoritism to you, or the other kids on the team will resent it. And when you make a mistake, I'll have to yell at you . . . even though another part of me might not want to."

"Yell all you want," I said.

"It's not as simple as that," Dad said.

"I still want to play for you. You're my dad."

Dad sighed and looked away, then gave my shoulder a squeeze. "I'll think about it," he said.

I felt bad right then, but I kept quiet.

When my dad says he'll think about something, it usually means *no.*

●　　●　　●

When I can't fall asleep, I start to imagine
I'm playing a ball game. I'm out on the
mound, of course, striking out guys one
after another.

I pitch to all the great hitters, and no one
can even hit the ball.

I want to be the best. I want to pitch for
the Hawks and win every game. I want my
dad to be so proud of me.

After that I'll play in Pony League, then in
high school, and then I'll be drafted in the
first round by a big league ball club.

A couple of years in the minors and I'll be starring in the major leagues. And when I am an immortal in the Hall of Fame, I can look back and say, "It all began when I pitched for my dad's team, the Hawks, and I was only ten years old."

5

Five-Hundred-Pound Gorilla

March turned right around and got warm. The temperature went up above fifty and the snow melted. It was a mess outside, with slush all over the streets and mud in the backyard.

That Saturday, really early, Dad took me down to the Kids Club. It was baseball registration day, and Dad had to help out. He's on the board of directors of the Kids Club now and goes to a lot of meetings at night.

It wasn't always called the Kids Club. It used to be the Boys Club, but then girls decided they wanted to play ball, too. So the people who run it changed the name.

Personally I wish that girls never got into playing baseball. Girls do nothing but mess up a team. They can't throw and they can't catch and some of them run funny. If they want, they should let girls have their own teams and play by themselves. With a softball.

A very soft ball.

I said all this to Mom once and she said I was a male chauvinist and was against girls and women. This is not true.

I have nothing against girls. After all, my mom is a girl, and I love her a lot. And I also think that girls should be allowed to be anything they want, including becoming doctors, lawyers, policemen, and even ditchdiggers if they like. Girls are people and should have equal rights with boys and men. And equal pay, like Mom says.

But there has never been a girl who grew up to be a major league ballplayer. Not one. So why should they play Mustang League ball and mess up everything by being slow, making errors, and not even knowing the game?

The Kids Club office is in Schenley Park, where all the ball fields are. When we got there, some parents and kids were already lining up outside.

We went inside the building and into the big room they use for registration. A few coaches and other people were there, and Dad said hello to them. Jack Sheridan, a friend of Dad's and a coach I knew, came over and shook my hand. Dad went off to get a cup of coffee.

"You're getting taller, Bobby," Mr. Sheridan said to me. "What is it, Mustang League for you this year?"

"Yep."

"How'd you like to play for me?" he asked.

"We've always got room on the Rangers for another good player."

"I'm not sure," I said. I felt a little embarrassed, if you want to know the truth. I wanted to play for my dad, but I didn't want to insult Mr. Sheridan.

"Maybe you'll play for the Hawks," said Mr. Sheridan. "I hear they've got a pretty fair manager."

"Pretty fair?" I said. "My dad is the best."

Mr. Sheridan started laughing as Dad came back with his coffee.

"Chuck," said Mr. Sheridan, "sounds like you've got Bobby brainwashed. I guess he wants to play for you."

"The age-old problem," said Dad.

"Yeah," Mr. Sheridan said. "Sometimes it works, sometimes not. I had to trade away my own kid a few years back. Every time I corrected Jay on the ball field, he took it personally. And brought it home with him. We started arguing at the dinner table. Neither one of us needed that."

Dad nodded and took a sip of coffee.

"If you don't want Bobby, just tell me," said Mr. Sheridan. "I'll be glad to have him."

"Thanks, Jack," Dad said. "I haven't made up my mind about it yet."

Dad and me sat down at one of the registration tables, and then they started letting people inside. It got so loud in the room I could hardly believe it. Kids were talking away a mile a minute, some were calling to friends, and parents were yelling at kids to keep quiet.

Everybody had to fill out a registration card with their name, age, and address on it. Parents had to make out a check or pay cash to the Kids Club. The cost was twenty-five dollars, and it was a deposit on the uniforms we would all get. At the end of the season the uniforms were collected and the parents could get their money back.

Dad said that a lot of parents didn't bother to get their money back and that money went to support the Kids Club.

I sat with Dad as parents and kids came by our table. My job was to keep an eye on the pens Dad brought with him. They had a way of disappearing into pockets.

Around noon Dad's work was done when another coach came along and took our place at the table. But before we left, I filled out a card of my own. The most important thing was your age. I put in my birthday, December 14th, and my age, 10¼. You had to be ten years old already, or become ten during the season, or you could not play in Mustang League.

Dad had to do some shopping for Mom on the way home. We drove to the big A & P on Beverly Road. I pushed the shopping cart. About halfway down the frozen food aisle I couldn't stand it any longer. "Look, Dad," I blurted out, "am I going to be on your team or not? Because I'm going bananas thinking about it."

Dad looked at me in surprise, a package of frozen french fries in his hand. "You're really worrying about it, aren't you?"

"You bet. Tell me yes or no."

Dad put the fries in the cart. "Okay," he said, "you can play for me."

"All right!" I said real loud.

"But," said Dad, pointing a finger at me, "let's get it straight from the get-go. I am the manager and you are a player. On the ball field, what I say goes. You got that?"

"Got it."

"If I say run three laps, you run three laps. No temper tantrums, no whining, no complaining."

"Okay."

"You'll call me skipper or coach, not Dad. And I never—ever—want to hear you say, 'Oh, Dad, please!' when we're on the field."

"Okay, okay," I said. "As long as you let me pitch."

"Hold it right there," said Dad. He put a big hand on my shoulder. "That's exactly what I'm talking about, Bobby. *I* decide where you play, not you. If I think you belong at second base or the outfield, that's where you'll play."

"But, Dad," I said, "I can be a great pitcher."

"Nobody's a pitcher on my team unless I tell them so, understand? You played second base and outfield in Learning League, didn't you?"

"Yes," I admitted, "but my arm's getting stronger. I know I could pitch. I've been training myself to pitch ever since I could pick up a baseball. You know that . . . you even put on your catcher's mitt and let me pitch to you a million times."

"Bobby," said Dad, "you don't throw hard enough."

"I'm bigger and stronger now," I said, a little louder, starting to get mad.

Dad raised his eyes to the ceiling and sighed. "Maybe you *should* play for Jack Sheridan," he said.

"Oh, Dad, please!" I said.

Dad looked at me, deciding. "Okay," he said, "on one condition. You've got to get it straight that I'm the boss. On the ball field I'm like a five-hundred-pound gorilla. What I say is law. Is that clear?"

"Yes. I understand all that."

"Me manager, you player," said Dad. "If I say faint, you close your eyes and fall to the ground."

"Yes, sir!" I said.

Dad didn't look exactly certain, but he nodded his head. "Okay," he said, "that's decided. Now, what do you want for dinner, chicken or steak?"

● ● ●

Me Manager, You Player
a story by Bobby "Baseball" Ellis

Sparky walked out to the bullpen. It was five minutes before his Tigers would play the hated New York Yankees. Big Jack, the Tigers' star pitcher, was warming up.

"Jack," said Sparky, "I've just changed my mind. You are not pitching today, you're playing first base."

Jack stared at his manager. "Wait a minute," he said, "I'm a pitcher. I'm the ace of the staff."

"First base," said Sparky.

"But I don't know how to play first base," said Jack.

"Me manager, you player," said Sparky. "First base is where you'll play."

"But Sparky," Jack said, "I get paid a million dollars a year to pitch. I'm one of the best there is at pitching."

"You'll play first base," said Sparky. "And by the way, Jack, tell your parents they must return your uniform at the end of the season or they won't get their $25 back."

6

"Jumpin'" Jason

Now I have to tell you about my best friend, Jason Moss.

Jason moved into a house down the street from me when I was four years old. We've been playing and hanging out together since then. In school Jason has always been in my class.

He's a great guy, and a funny one. Nothing ever seems to bother him. Jason is tall, almost a head taller than me, and he has red hair and a bunch of freckles across his nose and cheeks. He is also left-handed, which maybe explains why he sometimes acts like a ding-a-ling.

I was up in Jason's room and he had his stereo on, as usual. Jason is a music freak. He loves music even more than baseball, and his favorite group is Savage Towels. They had a new record out, and Jason was playing it and dancing to it for the twentieth time in a row.

"Kalarooty," sang Jason, "kazooty," which are all

the words to the song there are. I said Jason was dancing. It doesn't exactly look like dancing. What he does is to stick his arms out like a crazy bird and hop and jump from one foot to the other. It makes me think of a stork with a hot foot.

"Kazooty," I sang out with Jason. "Did you remember to register for Mustang League?"

"Oh, yeah," Jason sang back, "kazooty!" Jason jumped and spun in the air. "In the afternoon, with my dad. I looked for you but you were gone, kalarooty!" Now Jason began to play an imaginary guitar.

I told Jason all about how I got my dad to put me on the Hawks. I couldn't tell if he was listening or not.

With a final "kalarooty!" the song ended. "So are we going to be on the same team, or what?" Jason asked.

"I don't know," I said with a shrug.

"But your dad does," Jason said. He finally shut off the stereo and flopped down on the floor next to the bed, where I was sitting. "It'd be great if we kept playing ball together, like in Learning League. You at second base, me at first, the old combination together again, baseball fans."

"I'm going to pitch," I said.

"You're no pitcher."

"I can do it. I know it."

"The great Bobby Baseball," said Jason. "Throws like a chicken, hits like a turkey." Jason made a few chicken squawks. "Anyway," he went on, "I *will* be on the Hawks with you, right?"

"Don't ask me," I shrugged.

"We've got to be together," he said. "How could

they break us apart? It would be like bacon without eggs, like Bill without Cosby, like Savage without Towels, like—"

"Okay," I interrupted him.

"Like Cleveland without Indians, like Cincinnati without Reds."

"Jase," I said, "nobody knows what team they'll play for until they get a call from their manager. You know that's how it works."

"Yeah," said Jason, "except you already know you'll be playing for the Hawks, don't you?"

"Right."

"So why can't I play for the Hawks, too?"

"Maybe you will."

"Of course I will, dummy," said Jason. "Any manager in his right mind would want a player like me on first base. Tall, good range, a great glove . . . and a fantastic slugger."

"Who also lies a lot," I said.

"That too," said Jason with a grin. He jumped to his feet and took his batting stance. "Here comes the pitch," he said in his announcer's voice, "Jumpin' Jason Moss swings, and there's a long drive going out to the right-field fence . . . it's going, going, GONE!"

Now Jason trotted around the bases, waving to the imaginary crowd, tipping his imaginary cap as he crossed home plate, which turned out to be a spot near his dresser. "Another four-bagger," he said, flopping down near me on the floor.

"Looked foul to me."

"No way." He reached over, and we did a low five.

"So you're gonna run right home and talk to your dad, right? And he'll put me on the Hawks with you."

I was afraid that was coming, so I just stared at Jase.

"Come on," he said, "you know you'll do it."

"No, I don't."

"Yes, you do."

"Jase," I said, "were you listening when I told you how I had to practically beg him to put *me* on the Hawks? And how he said I had to never talk back to him and all that? So how can I turn around and ask him to put my friend on his team?"

"It's easy, dummy," said Jason. "You just go over to him, give him a big hug and a kiss, and say in your best voice, 'Oh, please, my wonderful father-manager, you must make sure that my best friend in all the world, the great Jumpin' Jason Moss, plays first base for the Hawks.' That's the way you do it."

"I don't know," I said.

"I don't believe this," said Jason, falling flat on the floor. "Are you afraid of your dad, or what?"

"I'm not afraid of him."

"Then just do it. What can happen? He'll get mad at you for a minute and a half? So what?"

"But it's just what Dad told me not to do," I said.

"Bobby," said Jason, "it's just a place on a ball team. It's not like I'm asking you to walk naked on Main Street, or rob a bank, or shoot your grandpa. Loosen up, will ya?"

"Okay," I said, although I didn't feel good about it. "I'll ask him."

"Now you're talkin'," said Jason. "Kalarooty!"

● ● ●

I was thinking about those ladies down in Haiti, sewing up new baseballs.

Suppose there was this one very old lady . . . and she was the one that stitched the ball that Roger Maris hit for his 61st home run, when he broke Babe Ruth's single season record?

And suppose that same old lady was the one who also stitched the ball Hank Aaron hit for his 715th home run . . . when he broke the Babe's all-time home-run record?

It could have happened. Maybe.

That would be amazing.

Would they put that old baseball-sewing lady in the Hall of Fame?

7

Not to Worry

"Fact of the day," Grandpa announced that Sunday morning at breakfast. We all looked up from eating.

"Mrs. Elvira Mason, of Burlington, Vermont," Grandpa read from the newspaper, "raised a zucchini in her garden that grew in the shape of the letter *W.* It weighed over four pounds."

"I hate zucchini," Sammy said.

"I love it," said Mom. "But I don't know if I'd like my vegetables to begin forming letters. Who knows where that could lead."

"They'd be great for alphabet soup," said Dad.

"Yes," said Mom. "But what happens if you get a salad that spells out, 'Don't eat me'?"

Dad started laughing and so did Sammy. "You crazy guys," he said.

I was glad to see Dad in such a good mood. Because I'd made up my mind to ask him about putting

Jason on the Hawks today. I didn't feel right about it, but I had to. Jason was my best friend, and I really wanted to play ball with him.

Jason has a way of keeping me cool because he never takes anything too seriously. Whenever I made errors, and I made lot of them before I learned how to get in front of a ground ball, I always got excited and angry. Jason can really calm me down when I get that way. He'll make a face or say something funny, and I start to laugh instead of blowing up.

"There are four ball games on cable this afternoon," Dad said.

"Oh, no you don't," said Mom. "This afternoon we are going to the movies."

"Aha," said Dad. "The mistress has spoken. Could it be that Tom Selleck has made a new picture?"

"No," said Mom, "just a film I think we should see."

"Your mother is madly in love with Tom Selleck," Dad said to Sammy and me.

"That I am," Mom said.

"In fact," said Dad, "if Tom Selleck should call, your mom would run away with him in a minute."

"You'd better hope he doesn't call," said Mom. "And after the movie, we are going out to dinner."

"Chinese?" asked Dad, "Italian?"

"Anywhere," said Mom. "I'm just announcing that this kitchen is closed for the day."

"Lithuanian? Albanian?" Dad went on. "Icelandic food, perhaps?"

"As long as they have burgers or spaghetti," Sammy said.

"And the movie isn't scary," I added. I hate those

horror movies where people are always getting carved up like turkeys. They give me the creeps. Sammy loves them.

We went out in the afternoon, except for Grandpa, who decided he'd rather finish reading his book. The movie was playing in the Grandview Mall, and it wasn't too bad. There was some love stuff in it, but it was pretty funny.

When we got back home, we all went to different places in the house. Mom picked up her book and sat down to read under the good lamp in the living room. Sammy trotted off to his room to work on his computer, as usual. Grandpa was napping in his room. And Dad went to his desk in the den to do some paperwork.

I started to follow Dad into the den to ask about Jason, but then I got scared and stopped. I went up to Sammy's room and asked him about it. "Do you think he'll get mad?" I said.

Sammy kept keying stuff into his computer. "Who knows?" he said. "Our dear father is sometimes hard to figure out."

"So what should I do?"

"Just do it," said Sammy. "The worst that can happen is he'll say no."

"Right," I said.

"Or he may just chop your head off," said Sammy.

"Thanks a lot."

Sammy looked up from his green screen. "I tried to tell you not to play for Dad, didn't I?" Sammy's smile was all I could see. His eyes were hidden behind his thick eyeglasses. "Oh, go ahead and do it," he said. "Be brave."

I took myself down to the den. Dad was writing stuff down on insurance forms. He was wearing the eyeglasses he only uses for reading.

"Could I talk to you a minute?" I asked him.

"Sure," he said, writing down a few more things. Then he took off his glasses and looked at me.

"This is about Jason," I began.

"Jumpin' Jason Moss," said Dad with a smile. "How is that young man?"

"Fine."

"I like Jason," said Dad. "He's a funny kid."

"And a good ballplayer."

Dad smiled again. "If you ask him about it, he is. That Jason is his own best publicity man."

"Well," I said, and my mouth seemed to go dry right then. "Uh," I said, "um . . . well. The thing of it is, Dad . . . you see . . . well . . . Jason asked me to ask you if he could play with me on the Hawks."

"Oh, Bobby," Dad said with a sigh.

I gulped and swallowed. I saw the disappointed look on Dad's face and I knew what was coming.

"This is just what we talked about," he said. "You're interfering with the team, aren't you? Because you're the manager's son. Asking for a favor for a friend. Isn't that right, Bob?"

I gulped again. "Yes," I said, "but it's only a little favor. Why can't Jason play on my team?"

"A little favor now, a bigger favor next time. Don't you see why it's wrong?"

"No," I said. I felt my cheeks getting hot. "We need players on the team. Why can't you let Jason be with me?"

"I won't do it, Bob," Dad said.

My temper was coming up, I could feel it.

"You could do it!" I blurted out, my voice getting loud like it always does when I get mad. "You just don't want to!"

"Cool off," Dad said in a warning voice.

But I was getting out of control. "It's not like I'm asking you something important," I said. "Why can't you let Jason be on the team?"

Dad gave me a long look, his eyes shooting into me like laser beams. "I'm not going to discuss it any further," he said in such a calm way that it only made me more angry. Then he put his glasses on again and began working on his insurance forms.

I looked at him for a minute, my hands balled up into fists. I began counting to ten in my head, trying not to start yelling like a madman.

Then I spun around and stomped out of the room as loud as I could.

● ● ●

I had a scary dream about playing ball.

I was on the mound, pitching. And every ball I threw got whacked for a hit.

I couldn't get anybody out.

I started yelling and screaming. Dad came out to the mound on the run. "I'm taking you out," he said.

I screamed at him. "No!"

"Yes. Give me the ball."

"No!"

"You're off the team," he said to me. "And you're not my son anymore."

8

Turnaround

I hated to tell Jason he wouldn't be on the Hawks with me. But I had to.

I just came out and told him when we were on the way to school the next morning. "I really tried to persuade my dad," I said, "but he wouldn't budge."

Jason was so cool he hardly made a face. "Your dad is dumb," he said. "He's losing out on an all-star first baseman. Maybe I should call him up and tell him how truly wonderful I am."

"I don't think that would help. When my dad makes his mind up, he's like a bulldog."

"Did you really try to persuade him?" Jason asked.

"Yes."

"Did you yell and scream and begin to throw things?"

"No," I said, "but I tried my best."

"Oh, well," said Jason. "I'll just have to hit all my home runs for some other team."

"I'm sorry, Jase."

"Me, too," he said. Then he started humming "Kalarooty" and we didn't talk anymore about it.

A few days later Dad went to a meeting of managers at the Kids Club. When he came home, Mom, Grandpa, and me were playing Scrabble in the kitchen.

Mom was winning, of course. She always wins at Scrabble because she knows every word in the English language. And even some that aren't in it.

Grandpa thinks Mom cheats and he is always challenging her. One time Mom dropped a *Z* on a triple letter score and made the word *zoril.* Grandpa challenged her, of course, but when he looked up the word in the dictionary, it turned out Mom was right again. Zoril is some kind of animal from Africa.

Mom's brain is totally awesome.

Dad came into the kitchen, poured himself a cup of coffee, and sat down with us. "Is she winning again?" he asked.

"Naturally," Grandpa said. "How'd your meeting go?"

"Fine," said Dad. "She's probably cheating," he told Grandpa.

"Of course she's cheating," Grandpa said. "When she doesn't have a word, she just makes one up."

"Oh contrair," said Mom in some foreign language. "I could beat this crowd with one brain tied behind my back."

Grandpa hooted out loud. "Listen to her," he said.

"My own daughter and she won't let me win a game sometime. The woman has no mercy."

Dad laughed and sipped his coffee. He took a pack of Mustang League registration cards out of his jacket pocket. "Looks like I've got a new bunch of Hawks this year," he said.

"Oh, wow!" I said, getting real excited. "Can I see?"

"Come on into the den," Dad said. When he got up, I followed him. He sat down in his desk chair. "Here you go," he said, and flipped the pack of cards to me.

I took off the rubber band and started looking at them. My card was right on top, then two kids I played with in Learning League: Karl Peters and Jackie Ulman. Behind those cards were those of some kids I knew from school: Jimmy Rossillo, Billy Alston, Michael Marder, and Nathaniel Robbins. The next two cards were girls, Jane DeMuth and Nancy Moriarty. The next registration card surprised me. "Jason!"

Dad nodded.

"Thanks!" I said and I jumped forward and threw my arms around Dad's neck in a hug.

"Whoa," said Dad as I backed off him. "That's what I wanted to talk to you about, Bobby. I did not—repeat not—ask for Jason to be on the Hawks. I want you to know that."

"But he's on the team, right?"

"Yes, he is," said Dad. "When we divided up the *B* players, Jason's card just came my way. I didn't ask for him. The only way he wouldn't be on the Hawks after that was if I traded him away. And that didn't seem right to me. So he's on the team, but not because you asked for him. Remember that."

"Okay," I said. I looked through the rest of the cards. I noticed that every card had a letter written in red pencil, *A, B,* or *C.* I asked Dad what those letters meant.

"That's our secret code," said Dad. "Coaches and managers grade the kids who've played for us. *A* is the best, *B* is an average player, and a *C* player needs to improve."

"But why do you do that?"

"We're trying to make teams of equal ability. It wouldn't be right for one team to have all the best players, like an all-star team."

"But who put down on my card that I'm only a *B* player?"

"The managers you played for in Learning League."

"Well, they're all wrong," I said. "I'm way better than an average player."

Dad smiled at me. "Maybe you are. We'll see. Your former coaches thought you were a good fielder, but your arm and your hitting need work."

"My arm is going to be great," I said. "What about Jason? Why is he only a *B* player, too?"

"Strikes out too much," said Dad.

"Yeah," I said, "but he can hit the ball a long way."

"When he hits it."

I looked at the cards again and noticed that we had five *A* players, five *B*'s, and five *C* players. I asked Dad if that's the way every team in Mustang League works.

"That's it," he said, "as close as we can make it. We all start out even-steven."

"Well," I said, "the Hawks are going to have an extra A player, me."

"Glad to hear it. Just play as well as you can and I'll be happy." Dad opened a bottom drawer in his desk and took out a bottle. "Time to get your glove in shape," he said. "Here's the neat's-foot oil."

When I took it from him, Dad grabbed hold of my wrist. "One more thing," he said. "Remember, you can't ask me for special favors because I'm your father. When practice begins, you're just another player to me. If I treat you differently, all your teammates will resent you. And I have to be fair to everyone, okay?"

"Okay."

"Promise me you'll behave."

"I'll behave," I said.

"Good," said Dad. "Go work on your glove."

I went off to the kitchen and called Jason on the telephone.

"Guess what?" I said. "You are now an official player on the Hawks."

"Kalarooty!" Jason said, sounding excited for once. "What happened? I thought he wouldn't put me on the team?"

"Well," I said, "Dad said he didn't do anything special. You were supposed to be on the Hawks anyway."

"That's great," Jason said. "Tell your father I love him."

"But maybe he did put you on the team. For me. Except he didn't want to admit it."

"What's the difference?" said Jason. "We'll be playing together."

"I know Dad likes you."

"Of course he does," said Jason, "I'm adorable."

"And crazy, too."

"Your dad is a wonderful man and I may marry him someday," Jason said.

I was laughing when I hung up the phone.

9

Baseball in
Your Mind

I took the neat's-foot oil up to my room and got my brand-new glove out of the closet.

I love that glove. It's a Willie Mays model and it fits my hand just right. The color of it is bright tan and the webbing is just a touch darker. I only put four fingers into it and it flexes really well.

I started working the neat's-foot oil into the pocket. The pocket of a baseball glove is the most important part because that's where the ball has to be caught. If the pocket is too stiff, the ball will pop out.

My glove's pocket is high up, and the webbing is part of it. The whole glove bends in half around a ball like a bun wraps around a hot dog. I oiled the pocket really well, then worked oil all over the fingers and the back of the glove, too. The glove looked a lot darker when I finished.

I got out my old baseball and popped it in and out

46

of the glove a few times. Then I walked in front of the mirror over my dresser and practiced my stretch move. A pitcher must have a good stretch move or base runners will keep stealing bases on him. I brought the glove up to my chest and held it there, peeked over my left shoulder at the mirror, then came forward in my throwing motion.

After a while I started making believe that a speedy runner was standing on first base, ready to steal on me. I held the stretch longer, staring at him over my shoulder. "You won't steal on me, pal," I said to myself, "no way."

That's when I heard someone chuckling, and Grandpa was standing in my doorway. "What inning is it?" he asked.

"No inning," I said, "I'm just practicing."

"Oh, pardon me," said Grandpa. "I thought you might be in the middle of a game."

"Sometimes I am," I said as Grandpa sat down in my desk chair.

"I know," he said. "I've seen you do it a hundred times."

"I usually pitch against the Cardinals or the Yanks or the Tigers. Sometimes I play out a whole World Series up here, with me pitching."

"So do I," said Grandpa, his head nodding up and down.

I couldn't believe it. "Grandpa," I said, "you really don't."

"Sure do."

"But you're so old," I said.

"What difference does that make? Sometimes when I'm lying in bed and I can't sleep, that's when I do it. I see myself out there standing on a pitcher's mound, a ball in my hand, getting ready to pitch. Then I start zippin' that old potato up to the plate. It's a much better way to fall asleep than counting sheep."

"Who do you pitch to?" I asked. "Which team, I mean?"

"The old Gashouse Gang, usually. The St. Louis Cardinals of '34 or '35, in around there. They were my team, you know, the one I really rooted for. Ol' Rip Collins, Pepper Martin, Joe Medwick, Dizzy Dean, those boys. I start in pitching to 'em, and by the time Medwick comes up, why I'm usually asleep. You don't ever want to pitch to Ducky Medwick, you know. That man could flat hit."

I stared at Grandpa for a minute. "It's hard for me to think of you doing that, Grandpa," I said. "I thought only kids like me did it."

"Who says I'm not still a kid?" said Grandpa with a smile.

"You still remember all those old players?"

"Can't ever forget 'em," said Grandpa. "Listen, Bobby, a real fan keeps the game in his head all his life. And if you ever played a little, like me, why it just never goes away."

I loved hearing Grandpa say that, and for a couple of seconds we just grinned at each other, sharing a secret.

"There's really two games of baseball," he said. "One gets played on the field and the other you play in your mind. Now, in the real game players will pop up and strike out and make errors and lose half the time. But the game in your mind is all your own, Bobby. You can hit home runs and steal bases and even strike out ol' Baby Ruth himself, if you like. That's the beauty part of it. Baseball in the mind, son. It's the best ball game there is, even for an old coot like me."

I handed Grandpa my glove and he popped the ball in and out of it a few times. "This is a great glove," he said, "and so *big*. When I played, we only used a little-bitty glove you could hardly fit all your fingers into." He popped the ball in the pocket one last time and handed the glove back to me. "Needs a touch more neat's-foot oil in the heel," he said.

"Where does neat's-foot oil come from?" I asked him.

"Beats me." He shrugged.

After a while Grandpa went off to bed and I worked more oil into the glove. Then I put the ball in the pocket, wrapped a few rubberbands around the glove real tight, and set it down on my bookshelf.

I kept wondering where neat's-foot oil comes from.

I know they must make it from some kind of animal. But what kind of animal is a neat?

And why do they only use its foot?

10

Practice . . .

When I got home from school Wednesday afternoon, Dad and Sammy were loading equipment into the station wagon for our first practice. I ran into the kitchen, grabbed a glass of milk and a cookie, then went upstairs and changed into my playing clothes. I wore old jeans, a sweatshirt, and because it was chilly, I put on an extra sweatshirt with a hood. I took my glove, left the ball on my desk, and ran out to the car. We picked up Jason down the street and took off for Schenley Park.

The Hawks were assigned to diamond number 5 as a practice field. It's sort of in a corner, away from the clubhouse. We took the equipment out of the car and carried it to the field. I grabbed a ball from the ball bag and began throwing with Jason. Sammy got the bases out and put them in place around the diamond.

Just when Jason and me were warmed up, Dad

looked over and called out to us, "Take it nice and easy! It's too cold to throw hard today."

Other kids started arriving. Sammy told Jason and me to sit down by the backstop. I said hello to the kids I knew from school: Nathaniel Robbins, Jimmy Rossillo, Michael Marder, and Billy Alston. When Dad got his clipboard and called the roll, only one kid was missing, Roger Tucker. Jackie Ulman said he was sick today and couldn't come.

Dad introduced himself and Sammy. Then he made a little speech about how a ball team must have a leader, and he was it. We had to listen to him and always do what he said. "Or else!" he added in a loud voice and kind of stared at us.

Nobody said anything except this girl sitting near me. "Or else what?" she piped up.

Dad looked surprised. "Or else you get benched, young lady."

"What's benched?" the girl asked, which was very dumb. Anybody who played Learning League ball knew what benched was.

"Benched means you don't play," said Dad.

"That's not fair!" the girl said.

I could see that Dad was annoyed. "Fair?" he said, really loud. "I decide what's fair or not. Remember that." He walked over to where she was sitting. "What's your name?" he asked her.

"Jane DeMuth."

Another girl alongside Jane spoke up. "Her name is DeMuth, but we call her Mouth."

Dad smiled. "Mouth, eh? You got that right."

Dad talked a little longer, explaining about batting helmets and safety. It was all stuff we knew from

Learning League, except when he asked who hadn't played Learning League ball, two kids raised their hands. One was a tall boy named Fred Miller, and the other was bigmouth Jane DeMuth, of course.

"Okay," said Dad, clapping his hands, "let's get warm. Two laps around the field."

We started jogging down the right-field line, following Dad, and he went pretty slowly so that everybody could keep up. It's a long way around a ball field when you run just inside the fence. By the time we finished our second lap, a lot of kids were huffing and puffing. Jane DeMuth was running next to me and Jason. She wasn't too tall and she had a ponytail sticking out from under her cap that kept bouncing up and down. "I love it," she yelled as we got near the backstop, "let's take another lap!"

Dad ignored that and got us lined up across the infield in two rows. Then he gave out baseballs to toss back and forth nice and easy. Jane was across from me, and we threw to each other. Dad walked around watching us, stopping now and then to show a player how to hold the ball, how to throw, and stuff like that.

My glove was soft as a pillow, and it was a good thing.

Because that Jane DeMuth was tossing the ball all over the place. Some bounced in front of me, others I had to jump to catch. She really had a funny way of throwing.

Dad came up behind her and watched for a minute. Then he stopped her. "Jane," he said, "you're throwing off the wrong leg."

He put his hands on her shoulders and turned her sideways. "Look," he said, "you're right-handed, so

you have to keep your right leg back when you throw and come forward with the *other* leg."

"But I never throw like that," Jane said.

"And that's why you've been throwing like a girl."

"But I *am* a girl!" Jane said. She looked insulted.

Dad started to laugh. "Sorry," he said, "but try it my way. And hold the ball with these two fingers and your thumb underneath, not with all five fingers."

Jane took the ball from Dad, gripped it like you're supposed to, and threw a perfect strike to me. "Wow!" she yelled, "that was really good."

When Dad finished watching everyone throw, he clapped his hands and sat us all down by the backstop again, out of the cold wind. Jason sat down next to me.

"Most kids think that hitting homers and scoring a lot of runs are the ways to win baseball games," Dad said. "Hitting is important, yes, but the real secret of teams that keep on winning is defense. Think about it: If you can keep the other team from scoring any runs, you can't lose, can you?"

"This team is going to win with defense," Dad went on. "That's pronounced de*fense,* not *dee*-fense."

Jason leaned over to me and whispered in his fake Mexican accent, "I heet dee ball over dee fence." I laughed out loud before I could stop myself.

Dad quit talking and glared a hard look at me. "Was there something funny in what I said?" he asked.

I felt my face get warm. "No, sir," I said.

"Something you'd like to share with us, Bobby?"

"No," I said.

"Ah," said Dad, "you're sure now?" Meanwhile,

everybody on the team had turned around to look at me.

"Yes, sir," I said in a cracked voice, feeling like a fool.

"Good," said Dad, and went on with his talk while I elbowed Jason in the ribs. Jase made a weird face at me, and I had to catch myself from laughing again. Dad was really sore at me, I knew that. He never spoke to me that way at home.

We practiced relay throws from the outfield, something we'd never done in Learning League. We were bad at first, with throws going every which way and kids dropping the ball. But then I think we got the hang of it.

The idea was to keep the ball moving fast and to drill the kid you were throwing to in the chest with the ball. Near the end of practice the ball was going from center to home pretty fast. And we weren't dropping too many balls, either.

It was getting dark when Dad put two fingers in his mouth and whistled real loud to call everyone in. "Same time, same place on Friday," he said. "Looking good, Hawks."

Jason and me rounded up the bases and balls and helped Sammy stow them away in the wagon. A few parents were waiting in cars parked near the field, and Dad made sure everyone had a lift home.

I had dinner, did my homework, and got into bed early. I was really tired, but it was a good kind of tired, from running and throwing and catching.

Dad came in to say goodnight and sat down on the edge of my bed. We looked at each other for a second, not speaking. Then I said I was sorry for laughing on the field.

"You should be," he said. "When I'm teaching the team out there, I don't need interruptions. Especially from my own son."

"It won't happen again," I said.

He frowned and looked away for a moment. "Bob, I don't want to be talking to you at home about something you did on the field. We get in trouble that way."

"I know," I said. "I hate this, too."

"I'm a different person on the ball field," he said. "Like a teacher. I don't want to have to be your father out there, okay?"

"Okay."

Dad reached over and mussed my hair. "What was so funny, anyway?"

I told him what Jason said, and Dad replied with a thin smile. "It's not that funny," he said. "I guessed it was either something Jason said or that girl, Mouth."

"I noticed you weren't as mad at her for interrupting you as you were at me," I said.

"Hold it," Dad said. "Let's not open that can of worms. I was a little easier on her because she's never played on a ball team before. Let's leave it at that."

"Girls are not ballplayers," I said. "Why do we have to let them play on the team?"

"Because it's fair," said Dad. "And because they deserve a chance to play ball if they want to."

"They stink," I said, "and they mess things up."

"Don't let your mom ever hear you say that," Dad said. He gave me a kiss, turned out the lights, and I went to sleep.

● ● ●

Girls should have their own league if they
want to play baseball.

They would have teams with names like
the Dollies, the Lipsticks, the Earrings, the
Pantyhose.

They would only play five-inning games,
so they wouldn't get tired.

They could stop after every inning and
have a tea party.

They would not wear baseball uniforms,
only dresses.

That's what I think and I don't care who
knows it, even my mom.

11

. . . Makes Perfect

The weather was warming up and so were the Hawks. I have to say this about Dad, even if he is my father: he is a very good manager.

We did not waste one single minute of practice. There was no goofing around. When the Hawks stepped on the field, we were all business.

Dad tried out everybody at different positions. He was fair, but very firm once he made his mind up. It was not like what I was used to back in Learning League. Back then everybody switched positions. You could play outfield one game and shortstop the next. We had eleven players on the field and we needed them all because nobody knew how to catch a ball.

The first thing Dad organized was the catching. He found a few kids who wanted to catch and worked with them. We had to have a good catcher behind the plate, Dad said, or every pitch would be a wild pitch.

Thank goodness I didn't want to be a catcher. I wouldn't take that job for a million dollars. It's the hardest, toughest, ugliest job on a ball team.

First of all, you've got to play with all this equipment that weighs you down. A hard helmet, a mask that goes over your face, a chest protector that goes from shoulders to waist, and shin guards that buckle around your legs. I once put on all that stuff and I could hardly move. And even if you can move around, you've got the batter swinging a bat right in front of your face and foul tips hitting you.

Sammy played catcher. I remember how he would come home from games and have these black-and-blue bruises all over his arms where he got hit by foul tips.

I don't think it's so great to get banged up every game.

By the end of the second week of practice the catchers were picked. I knew both of them from school, but we weren't friends. One was Jimmy Rossillo. He was a tough kid, always getting in trouble in school for fighting. The other kid was really fat. His name was Ned Robbins, but other kids called him Jelly Belly. Ned was so big around he could hardly run at all. In fact, you could send out for a pizza and get it delivered in the time it took Ned to circle the bases.

Dad put Sammy in charge of the catchers, and every practice he would put Jimmy and Ned in front of the backstop and throw balls at them really hard.

The rest of the team Dad divided into outfield and infield. Naturally Jason and me were infielders. It was clear from the start that Jase was best at first base.

And I was the best second baseman, even if I do

say so myself. I wasn't afraid to get in front of a ground ball and grab it. Behind me was Mouth, Jane DeMuth. She had a lot to learn about playing infield, but she tried hard. One day a ground ball came up and hit her right in the mouth. She yelled out, but then turned around and ran after the ball. When she got it, we could all see her mouth was bleeding.

Dad came running over to Mouth as all the infielders gathered around. "I'm okay," Mouth said. "Let's keep playing ball."

But Dad wouldn't let her. He held her face and looked into her mouth. "Let's make sure you haven't knocked any teeth loose," he said.

They weren't, but her lip was split and it kept bleeding.

Dad turned to me. "Get a towel out of the duffel bag and get it wet," he ordered.

I ran to the bench and found a towel. Then I had to go about a half a mile to the nearest drinking fountain. I ran all the way there, got the towel soaking wet, and ran all the way back.

Dad had Mouth off to the side when I got back.

"I'm fine," she said. "I want to keep practicing."

Dad wrung out the towel and put it to Mouth's mouth. "You just sit here and keep that towel on your lip," he said. "And that's an order."

And that's how Mouth sat out the rest of practice, holding that wet towel to her lip. It was the only time since I'd met her that she stopped talking.

As much as I didn't like girls on the team, I have to say this about Mouth. She was really brave and tougher than some guys I could name.

She didn't even cry once.

At home I kept asking Dad when he would get around to picking out the pitchers. "Soon," was all he would say, "and don't be a pest about it."

One night at dinner I was telling Grandpa about how great I could be if I ever got the chance to pitch. Grandpa winked at Dad. "I think the boy fancies himself a hurler," he said.

"I got the message," Dad said. He took a sip of his coffee and looked at me over the cup. "Bob, the team could use you at second base. You could be really important out there on defense."

"Other kids can play second," I said. "Mouth is getting pretty good. But I would be the best pitcher the Hawks could have, you know that's true."

"I'm not at all sure of that," he said. "Jack Ulman could probably pitch. He's left-handed and has a strong arm."

"You know Jackie is going to back up Jason at first base," I said. "I heard you tell him that."

"That kid who didn't play in Learning League," Dad said, "what's his name? Fred Miller. He could probably pitch."

"Fred Miller!" I said, starting to get hot. "He makes so many mistakes! He doesn't even know the game, Dad. If a ball came back to him on the mound, he wouldn't know what to do with it."

"I like Freddie," said Dad. "He doesn't say much, but he has a lot of talent and a great arm. I could probably teach him to pitch."

"Come on," I said.

"Tony Gomez has a good arm," said Dad, "Mike Lum—"

"I give up!" I said. "You've got the best pitcher

in the whole Mustang League right here in your family—"

Sammy gave a loud hoot at that.

"—and you won't let him pitch. It's downright unfair!"

"Even Mouth can throw pretty well now that she knows how," said Dad. "That girl is a pistol."

That's where I lost my head.

"Her?" I yelled. "A girl?" I jumped up from the table and threw my napkin down. Sammy began to laugh at me and I made a face at him. Then I turned around and ran up the stairs to my room.

I sat down on my bed and tried to cool off. After a moment I got my baseball and began tossing it in my hand.

Sammy came in. "Why do you have to be such a baby?" he said. "Couldn't you tell that Dad was just teasing you a little?"

"He wasn't teasing," I said. "He means it."

"No, he doesn't," said Sammy. "He was just getting back at you for being a pest about pitching."

"Am I the best pitcher, or not?"

"Probably not," said Sammy, and when I stuck out my tongue at him, he smiled. "Maybe you are, I don't know. You arm isn't too strong, but maybe you can fool them with your slow stuff."

"I throw strikes, don't I?"

"Yeah," Sammy admitted, "that you do. You've got good control."

"Then why won't Dad let me pitch?"

"He probably will give you a chance, Sneezer. But not if you carry on like a crazy kid. A pitcher has to be calm, you know, not blow up like a nickel firecracker. If you'll just be cool, fool, Dad will try you on the mound."

"No, he won't," I said. "He practically said I was going to play second base. And he seems to think almost anybody else is better at pitching—even a stupid girl!"

"Calm down," Sammy said. He sat down on the bed beside me. "Dad is all business about baseball, you know. The team comes first with him. Not the player. Not even his son."

"I know that."

"In the end he'll give you a chance to pitch," said Sammy. "But you've got to show him you're the best. Not by carrying on and throwing tantrums. Got that?"

"Yeah," I said.

"Okay."

I flipped my baseball up, and Sammy reached out and grabbed it. He began to turn it around in his hand.

"Dad can be strange, sometimes," said Sammy after a moment. "He can be hard to play for."

"I know."

"Not yet you don't," Sammy said. "Did I ever tell you why I became a catcher?"

"Because you wanted to be."

"Wrong," said Sammy. "Last thing I wanted to be was a catcher. But we didn't have anyone good who volunteered. And I was a pretty good ballplayer. So Dad said, 'Sammy? How about you give catching a try?' And he started teaching me how to catch."

"And you loved it," I said.

"Wrong again," said my big brother. "I hated it.

Every game I got myself banged up, hit every which way by foul tips, balls bouncing in the dirt. I even got knocked silly by a bat one time. I hated it."

Sammy's face was so serious. I knew he wasn't kidding around.

"So why did you catch if you hated it?" I asked.

Sammy shrugged. "The team needed me. And my own dad wanted me to. I don't know, it just seemed like I had to do it. I didn't want to let Dad down, I guess."

Neither one of us spoke for a while. Sammy kept turning my baseball, and I kept looking at him. And I felt sorry for Sammy right then. If I was forced to be a catcher, I'd probably quit the team.

"Now you see why it's better not to play for your old man," Sammy said. "People think it's easier, but it's not. It's way, way harder to play ball and please your dad at the same time."

Sammy stood up, stretched, and flipped my ball back to me. Then he went off to work on his computer. I washed up and went to bed. But I couldn't get what Sammy said out of my mind.

I loved Dad. I wanted to please him. But if he didn't give me a chance to pitch . . . I didn't want to think about that.

● ● ●

I finally found out where neat's-foot oil comes from.

Mom made me look it up in her huge dictionary when I asked her about it.

I found out that "neat" is a word that means an animal of the cow family.

Neat's-foot oil is made by boiling up the foot bones and shinbones of cows.

I think that's gross and I'm sorry I looked it up.

12

On the Mound

Dad didn't tell me—or anyone—that he was going to have a pitching tryout until he did it.

It was the beginning of the last week of practice before the real season began. The team was pretty well set by then. Mike Lum was playing third base, Tony Gomez was at shortstop. Jase was at first, of course, with Jackie Ulman backing him up. I was first-string second base, which sounds funny. Behind me was Mouth and Tuck, Roger Tucker. Karl Peters, who we all called KP, was a kid who could fill in at all the infield positions except first base.

The outfield was set as well. Freddie Miller was great in center, Mike Marder and Billy Alston played left and right. A few other outfielders were okay, except for Nancy Moriarty, Mouth's friend, who couldn't play at all. She couldn't catch a fly ball except by luck; she couldn't hit or throw or run. Besides that, she stunk. I said that about Nancy to Dad one night at home and he laughed. "Everybody gets to play at least half the game," he said. "Those are the rules. It doesn't matter how bad you are; if you want to play, you will."

Dad ended practice a little early. When we gathered at the bench, he said, "I want Mike Lum, Tony Gomez, Fred Miller, and Bobby Ellis to stay for a while."

The other kids began leaving. Sammy put on a catcher's mitt and got behind the plate. Dad led the four of us out to the mound. "I think you kids have some pitching talent," he said. "You can play other positions as well, but we do need a couple of pitchers on this team."

I almost laughed out loud at that. "A couple of pitchers?" I'd heard Dad say pitching was ninety percent of the game about a zillion times. So why was he making it sound like it wasn't important?

Dad handed the ball to Tony Gomez and told him to throw a few pitches to Sammy. Tony hesitated, then gave Dad a smile. "I'd really like to play shortstop," he said. "If it's all the same to you, Mr. Ellis."

"Give it a try anyway, Tony," said Dad.

Tony shrugged, then stepped up on the hill. He began to throw to Sammy as we all watched. He was okay, but wilder than me, of course.

Mike Lum was next to try out. And he had bad control. Mike threw the ball in the dirt more times than he threw it into Sammy's mitt. "Fine," said Dad as he took the ball from Mike.

"Maybe I'd better stick to third base," Mike said.

"Okay," said Dad, "but I want you to throw batting practice sometimes. You've got a good arm, Mike." Then Dad turned around to Fred Miller. "Freddie, show me how you pitch," he said.

Freddie took the ball and got up on the rubber. For a second he didn't quite know what to do, how to stand or wind up, where his feet should go. Dad went over and demonstrated for Freddie, then showed him how to grip the ball. Freddie looked a little scared, but he began to pitch a few.

I have to say this about Freddie Miller's arm: It was a gun. The few times he managed to hit Sammy's glove, he really made it pop. But Freddie looked clumsy throwing the ball. He slipped a few times and the ball flew over Sammy's head and ponged off the backstop.

"Okay," Dad said and took the ball from Freddie.

"I wasn't so hot," Freddie said.

"You just need some work," Dad said. He told Freddie that he would be a batting-practice pitcher, too. Then he turned to me.

"Okay, Bob," Dad said, "show me something."

I should have been nervous, but I wasn't. This was the moment I had been thinking about, planning on, dreaming about for years. I knew in my heart I was great. Now all I had to do was show it.

I stepped up on the rubber. Behind the plate Sammy was grinning at me. He pumped his fist into his mitt then held that fist to his heart. Be strong, Sammy was saying; do it.

What I had in my head was what I'd heard over and over from Dad: "Throw strikes."

And I did.

Every ball I threw caught a part of the plate. Noth-

ing wild, nothing in the dirt, nothing Sammy even had to get out of his crouch for.

"Good control," Dad said from behind me. "Can you put a little more zip behind it?"

I started throwing harder, and the ball began to stay up, too high.

"Don't overthrow," Dad said.

I went back to my normal way of throwing and kept the ball in the strike zone. Maybe I wasn't as hard a thrower as Mike and Tony—I sure couldn't throw as fast as Freddie—but I knew where the ball was going, that's for sure.

"Okay," Dad said from behind me. I turned around.

"We'll give you a shot," Dad said. "You can be our starting pitcher."

When I heard Dad say that, I really wanted to start yelling and screaming and jumping up in the air. But I controlled myself. I just couldn't stop grinning, that's all. "Great," I said. "I'm going to be fantastic, skipper. I'm never going to lose a game, not one."

Dad began to laugh. "One thing I can see," he said. "You sure don't lack confidence."

We walked off to the bench and began packing up the equipment. I was so pumped up, I ran around the bases and gathered them as I went. Then I ran back to help put all the stuff into the wagon. Sammy and me loaded and Dad got in front to drive. "All right," said Sammy. He gave me a big hug. "You showed him something."

I felt like I'd just won the last game of the World Series.

● ● ●

The Last Game
by Bobby "Baseball" Ellis

Top of the ninth inning, two out, two
strikes on the batter. The Cardinals were
down to their last strike. One more out and
the Tigers would win the World Series.

I looked in to my catcher crouched behind
the plate, Slug McGurk. He put one finger
down, fast ball. I shook him off. Slug went
to two fingers, the curve. I shook him off
again.

Slug called time and came running out to
the mound, his mask in his hand. "Do you
want to waste a pitch?" he asked me.

"No need for that," I said. "I'll throw the
scroogie."

"You sure?"

"This batter is out," I said, "except he
doesn't know it yet."

And that's how I fanned the batter and
became the winning pitcher in the final
game of the Series. Best screwball in
the game since Carl Hubbell, that's what
people say.

I know some people call me a show-off, a hot dog, and a bragger. But when you've got stuff like I have, that's not bragging—that's confidence.

13

By the Numbers

"Fact of the day," Grandpa announced that Saturday morning at breakfast. He read from the newspaper. "North America's longest suspension bridge is the Verrazano–Narrows Bridge connecting Brooklyn and Staten Island in New York City. The span is four thousand two hundred sixty feet long, exceeding the Golden Gate Bridge in San Francisco by sixty feet."

"What's the third longest bridge?" I asked him.

"Doesn't say," said Grandpa. "Could be the bridge in my mouth that goes from my last molar to my eyetooth."

"Fact of the day is we've got to start moving out of here to practice," Dad said.

"And after practice we get our uniforms," I said.

We had a terrific practice that morning. I tossed batting practice, nice and easy like Dad said. I just put the ball over the plate and let kids hit it. Ned Robbins and Jimmy Rossillo took turns behind the plate, with Sammy standing by to coach them. Dad was up at home plate, too, correcting kids' swings. We worked on bunting too, which is harder than it looks.

Jimmy was really good at coming out from behind the plate, grabbing a bunted ball, and firing it down to Jase at first base. Ned Robbins was terrible. He was slow and had trouble bending down and grabbing the ball.

Then Dad put Mike and Freddie up on the mound with me, and we all had to practice running over to cover first on a ball hit to Jason. Dad said that a pitcher had to make this play so often, he should be able to do it in his sleep.

Practice was over about 1:00 P.M. Sammy went off with some friends. It was time for the team to walk over to the clubhouse and pick up our uniforms.

The Hawks uniform is a light blue color with red stripes on the sleeves and down the side of the pants. *Hawks* was written in red script across the front of the shirt, and the number on the back was red as well. The cap is dark blue with a red bill and red letter *H* on the front.

On the way to the clubhouse Dad handed me his clipboard. "I've got a little job for you," he said. I was to write down the uniform number each player would get next to the player's name on the sheet. And I was also supposed to record each player's nickname.

"What for?" I asked Dad.

"The Kids Club prints rosters to use in games," he said. "And we also make up souvenir programs that we sell to raise money."

Dad went inside the clubhouse to do some work.

The rest of us Hawks waited by the door to be called. Finally a coach stuck his head out the door and called us in.

Hawks uniforms were stacked on a long table, and there were coaches behind the table helping kids find their proper size. I went to the end of the table, where the caps were stacked up.

Jason was the first to get his uniform and cap. "I got number seven," he said, "which is lucky."

"That's Mickey Mantle's old number," I said, writing it on the sheet. "What do you want for your nickname?"

"Need you ask? 'Jumpin' with no *g*, of course."

I wrote it down next to Jason's name.

Fred Miller got number three, which was Babe Ruth's number. When I asked him what nickname he wanted, he spoke so low I could hardly hear him.

"Don't have one," he said.

"You've got to."

"Freddie, I guess."

"You could make one up," I told him. "How about Moose or Goose?"

Freddie shrugged. "Freddie."

I wrote it down. There have been some players called Freddie, like Valenzuela and Lynn. But Goose is a great nickname.

I could hear a loud voice yelling, and it was Mouth shooting her mouth off again. "I don't want that stupid number!" she was saying to the man behind the table who was handing her a shirt.

"What's wrong with four?" the man asked.

"I want a double number," said Mouth. "Twenty-two or thirty-three, or something like that."

"But I don't have a number like that in a small enough size."

"You haven't looked through the whole pile," Mouth insisted, her voice going up like a siren.

"Take the shirt," the man said.

"I won't!" said Mouth. "Four is a stupid number. Why don't you let me look through the whole pile until I find what I want?"

The man behind the table shook his head. "Be my guest, girlie," he said. "Look as long as you like, but you gotta be outta here in ten minutes."

Anthony Gomez came by with number 14 and he wanted his nickname to be Tony. Karl Peters got 23 and his nickname was KP. Michael Marder got 34 and was called Mike. Sean Gardner got uniform number 43 and said he didn't have a nickname but kids called him Gardy. I wrote *Gardy* on the sheet.

Then Nancy came along with Mouth right behind her. Mouth finally got a shirt she wanted, number 11. "And your nickname is Mouth," I said.

"No, it's not," she said, which surprised me.

"Then what is it?" I asked her.

"My nickname is Janie," she said.

Nancy started giggling. "You know we all call you 'Mouth.' What's this Janie business?"

Mouth's face got all serious. "Janie happens to be what my mother calls me. That is my nickname, whether you like it or not."

"Mouth is your nickname," Nancy said.

"It is not!" Mouth insisted.

I probably shouldn't have said anything, but I did. "I think Janie is a dumb name for a ballplayer."

"Who asked you?" said Mouth, swinging around to glare at me.

"Mouth is a much better baseball name," I said.

"Oh, yeah?" said Mouth. "Well, I don't think so. I don't care if my friends call me Mouth, but I don't want people I don't even know calling me that."

"It is your real nickname, though," said Nancy. "You can't deny it."

"It is," I agreed.

Mouth shook her head, and her ponytail flew around. "Some people who used to be my friends started calling me that because they say I talk too much. But I know that I don't. And I don't have a big mouth, either."

"Yes, you do," said Nancy.

"Yeah," I added, "you really do talk a lot, Mouth."

"Well, thanks a lot," said Mouth, looking insulted. She put her lips together for a second and blew some air out. "What's *your* nickname?" she asked me.

"Baseball," I said. "Bobby Baseball."

Mouth's face broke into a grin. "You're kidding me, right?"

"No."

"Bobby Baseball?" said Mouth. "I wouldn't call you that in a million years."

"You don't have to," I said, "but it's still my nickname."

"It sounds so stupid!" Mouth declared in her loudest voice.

"It's not stupid, it's great!" I said.

"Sheesh!" said Mouth. "Bobby Baseball? One of the dumbest names of all time."

Now I was the one starting to get mad. "Look," I said, "your nickname is Mouth, whether you like it or not. That's what I'm writing down."

"Come on, Mouth," said Nancy. "Everybody's been calling you Mouth since kindergarten. Even Coach calls you Mouth now. So what's the big deal?"

"All right, all right!" Mouth yelled. "If Bobby can have a stupid nickname, then I can have one, too." She put her Hawks cap on her head sideways so it looked really goofy. "Bobby Baseball, huh?" she said to me. "That is really ridiculous."

She and Nancy walked away, and I wrote down Mouth next to her name on the list. Then I underlined it twice just to make sure.

When all the Hawks had their uniforms and I had their nicknames and numbers, I went and got my own uniform, number 9, which was fine with me.

Ted Williams wore number 9, and he became an immortal.

●   ●   ●

I looked up Ducky Medwick in one of Dad's old baseball books. He was a terrific hitter, just like Grandpa said. One year Ducky Medwick won the National League batting title, and he still holds the St. Louis Cardinals runs batted in record: 154. That was one run a game knocked in back then.

Medwick's real name was Joseph, or Joe. Some people called him Muscles. How he got the nickname Ducky was when some girls thought he was cute and they started calling him Ducky-Wucky.

Someday I hope the name Bobby Baseball will be as famous as Ducky Medwick.

It sure sounds better than Ducky.

14

Asleep on the Mound

Spring was getting springier and a lot warmer. I started wearing my lighter jacket to school. One day I just wore a sweater over my shirt.

At practice a lot of kids were starting to hit the ball better. It was way different from Learning League. Back then we hit the ball off a tee our first year. After that our own coaches tossed the ball to us underhanded and easy. Even so, some kids never managed to hit the ball.

Jason cut down his swing a lot under Dad's teaching. Now he hit line drives sometimes. Ned Robbins could hit the ball a mile, when he hit it. Even I was getting better. I hit some sharp grounders now that might even have found holes and been hits.

In the last week of practice before the games began, Dad decided that we would play a squad game. Us against us.

We didn't have enough players for nine on a side, but Dad said that didn't matter. I was pitching for one team, Freddie for the other.

Dad stood just behind me on the mound to umpire. Jimmy was my catcher. For the first time on the mound, I felt really nervous. Then Nancy Moriarty led off and waved her bat at three pitches. One out. I felt better already.

Jackie Ulman got up. I threw one down the middle; Jackie swung and hit an easy bouncer between the mound and first base. I watched as Jason ran over and grabbed it. But when he looked to toss the ball to me covering first base, I was still standing on the mound. Jackie was safe at first.

"Time!" Dad called. He took the ball from me and rubbed it in his hands. "What are you, a spectator!" he yelled at me. "You're supposed to cover first base! Automatically! In your sleep! This is stupid baseball!"

I felt about as big as a peanut and twice as dumb. I shuffled my feet and stared at the ground. All the kids on the team were watching me, and I felt embarrassed enough to die.

"You want to watch the game, go sit in the stands!" Dad yelled at me in a voice you could hear in the next county. "You want to play ball, keep your head in the game!"

He handed the ball back to me, and I couldn't look him in the eye. I felt ashamed and angry at myself. I knew what I should have done on that play. I just didn't do it.

I don't want to write any more about the game because it was completely horrible. I put it down in my memory book as a game to forget.

The squad game was way different from practice. It was real. Kids were running out the balls they hit. You had to catch a batted ball and throw someone out. You had to stop a kid from stealing a base, which nobody could do. We stunk on ice, all of us on both teams.

The only good thing was that Freddie pitched worse than me. He couldn't find the strike zone with a road map. And Ned, his catcher, kept going to the backstop to pick up wild pitches.

After everyone had batted for both teams, Dad stopped the game and made us all sit down by the bench. He didn't say anything for a minute, he just kept walking back and forth, his hands behind his back. We didn't need a seeing-eye dog to tell us how angry he was.

"Who are you people?" he roared at us. "Is this a kindergarten team out here? You're sure not the Hawks I've seen practicing for three weeks!"

Dad took another walk, shaking his head.

"Baseball is a simple game, people. You catch, you throw, you hit. AND YOU THINK!

"I will not yell at anyone for making an error. Everyone makes errors. BUT I WILL NOT PUT UP WITH MENTAL MISTAKES!"

In the next hour we went back to basics, drilling and drilling on the things we forgot to do in the squad game. Relays, cutoffs, holding runners on base, backing up other players, base running, double plays. Dad wasn't smiling at all. He didn't give anyone a compliment, like he usually did when one of us did something right. It was all serious, and none of it was much fun.

Finally he let everyone go home. Except for me. Dad got the ball bag and stood near home plate. I had to be on the mound. Then Dad rolled a ball between first base and me, and I had to break for first base and run over there. I did it time after time after time, until two dozen balls were lying in right field. Then I had to get the ball bag and go pick them all up.

When I did that, I brought the ball bag to Dad. "What do you do when a ball is hit to the right side?" he asked me.

"I cover first base."

"Do you think about it when the ball is hit?"

"No, I start running to first base."

"Right," said Dad. "Let's do it some more."

I looked over at Sammy, who was sitting by the backstop. He turned his head away.

I ran over to cover first base three ball bags' worth. Six dozen times. I was so tired when we finished, I could hardly bend over and pick up the balls. But Sammy came over to help. "Great game, isn't it?" he said real low so that Dad couldn't hear.

"Is Dad always so mean to his players?"

"No," said Sammy. "Only to his sons."

"I hate him when he's like this," I said.

"Join the club," said Sammy.

It was almost dark as we gathered the equipment and put it into the duffel bags. Nobody spoke much on the way home. I was too mad to trust my mouth. I was afraid I'd say something to make Dad madder than he was.

When we got home, I helped Sammy put the equipment into the garage. Then I went upstairs and took a long shower. I was really tired and I felt beat up. I just picked at dinner. Even Grandpa's silly stories didn't cheer me up.

I went right up to my room after dinner and did my homework. Let me not lie; I did *most* of my homework and skipped the rest. Then I did my go-to-bed things and got under the covers. It was only nine o'clock when I shut off the light.

Of course I rolled around in bed and couldn't fall asleep.

I kept thinking back to the afternoon . . . the look on Dad's face . . . the sound of his voice. He'd never spoken to me like that in my whole life. Okay, I made a mistake, that was true. But I was the one he was toughest on. It was only me he yelled at that way and embarrassed. Other people made mistakes too, but he was a lot easier on them.

It was unfair, I thought, and that thought gave me a bad feeling down in my stomach. It looked like Dad planned on being harder on me than on the other kids. And lying there in my bed in the dark, I began to figure out why.

I was his son and he expected more of me.

I was his son and I wanted to do better for him.

He was my Dad, so he could yell at me more.

He was my Dad, so it hurt me more when he did.

It all kept going around and around in a circle. Why did it make me feel like crying?

● ● ●

I only know two fathers who managed their sons in the major leagues. Yogi Berra had his son Dale play for him on the

Yankees. Cal Ripken, Sr., managed his sons Billy and Cal Ripken, Jr., for a while.

I wonder how much those guys yelled at their sons.

15

Mister Cluck

Practice wasn't so much fun anymore.

Dad was making everyone crazy, especially me. "Hustle!" he kept yelling at me. "Think!" One day I failed to go behind third base to back up Mike. I had to run three laps around the field.

I cut down on my mistakes, but Dad kept after me. It was like I was Mister Cluck on the team, the stupid one. I hated every second of it when he singled me out and yelled at me in front of everyone. He didn't yell that way at Mouth, and she made plenty of mistakes. He didn't say a word to Jimmy when he didn't hustle down to first on a batted ball. Jimmy wouldn't take that yelling from Dad. He was so tough, he might even pop Dad one.

One day after school I went over to Jason's house to hang out. I was feeling mad about Dad and I said so.

"He's using me to yell at and I know why, Jase. Because I'm his son and I won't talk back."

"This is true," said Jason, who was connecting Legos on the floor.

"It's unfair, isn't it?"

Jason connected a couple more pieces. What he was constructing looked totally weird. "Well, it could be a good thing," he said.

"What's good about it?"

Jason didn't answer. He kept pulling Legos apart and then reconnecting them. I asked what he was making. "Don't know yet," he said. "Either a rocket or a giant sour pickle."

"So what's good about it?" I repeated.

"Look at it this way," he said. "Nobody on the team can say you get better treatment because you're his son."

I hadn't thought about that. It still didn't seem right to me.

"I just wish he'd treat me like other kids. Treat us all the same."

"That's what my dad says about his boss," said Jason. " 'He treats us all exactly the same—like dogs.' "

Later that night Dad came home from a meeting at the Kids Club. I was writing in my baseball book when he came into my room.

"The roster cards are printed," he said. "I thought you'd like to see one."

I took a card from him and looked it over. "Great," I said, but I know my voice didn't sound too excited.

Dad stood there. "Is that all? I thought you'd be jumping up and down."

Kids Club Mustang League

HAWKS

Sponsored by ALMAC HARDWARE; 17th and Main
For All Your Home Needs

Number	Player	Throws	Bats	Position	Nickname
30	William Alston	R	R	OF	Billy
11	Jane DeMuth	R	R	2B	Mouth
9	Robert Ellis	R	R	P	Baseball
43	Sean Gardner	L	L	OF	Gardy
14	Anthony Gomez	R	R	SS	Tony
5	Michael Lum	R	R	3B	Mike
34	Michael Marder	R	R	OF	Mike
3	Frederick Miller	R	R	OF	Freddie
16	Nancy Moriarty	L	L	OF	Nan
7	Jason Moss	L	L	1B	Jumpin'
23	Karl Peters	R	R	IF	KP
21	Nathaniel Robbins	R	R	C	Ned
15	James Rossillo	R	R	C	Jimmy
36	Roger Tucker	R	R	IF	Tuck
25	John Ulman	L	L	IF	Jackie

Manager: Charles "Chuck" Ellis
Coach: Samuel "Sammy" Ellis

Schedule:	JAYS	April 2	TIGERS	May 7
	at LIONS	April 10	LIONS	May 14
	at TIGERS	April 17	at BANKERS	May 22
	BANKERS	April 23	at JAYS	May 27
	RANGERS	April 30	at RANGERS	June 4

all games played at SCHENLEY PARK
23rd and Schenley Ave.

SUPPORT KIDS CLUB BASEBALL ! ! ! PATRONIZE OUR SPONSORS ! ! !

ALMAC HARDWARE
17th and Main
Proprietors: Al Foster
Mac Foster

"It's fine," I said. I put the roster card down on my desk.

"Right," said Dad. He came closer and rubbed my hair. "Is there anything wrong, Bobby?"

"Nope." I started writing in my book again.

"Something you want to talk over with me?"

I started to open my mouth, then thought better of it. I wasn't a complainer. And I wasn't going to show Dad I was a crybaby, either. "Nope," I said.

Dad stood for a second, looking at me. "Okay, champ," he said. "First game is this Saturday, against the Jays. You know who's pitching for us?"

"Me, probably."

"You got it."

"My first no-hitter," I said. "I'll probably strike out fifteen."

"Let's just win it, okay?" When Dad left, I picked up the roster card and started getting excited. It looked terrific.

I stuck the roster card in the back of my baseball book. The first team I would ever pitch for. The start of my long and great career on the mound. You better believe I was going to save it.

When I got into bed, Mom came in. She sat down on the bed and gave me a kiss on the forehead. "Is everything okay with you, kiddo?" she asked me.

"Yeah."

"You didn't say two words at dinner tonight. And you've got that sorrowful look in your eyes. What's bothering you?"

"Nothing."

"Come on, honey," she said, "you can't fool your old mom."

I wanted to tell her about Dad and me, but then I didn't want to tell her. It was between Dad and me. So I just kept my mouth shut.

"Speak, oh great sphinx," she said, then looked at me for a minute. I kept still. "Strong, silent type, eh? It must be really bad."

I knew Mom wouldn't give up until I said something. That's the way she is sometimes, like a detective. So I said, "It's something between Dad and me, that's all. About how he treats me on the field."

"Oh, dear," she said, and sighed.

"Please don't say anything to Dad about it."

"We'll see," she said. "You know, sweetie, there are only a few things your dad is a perfectionist about. And baseball is one of them. Please remember that Dad doesn't mean anything by it. He just knows how the game should be played and he gets aggravated."

"You can say that again," I said, which made Mom smile.

"It's a game, honey, only a game. It's not life or death."

"It's very important to me," I said. "I'm going to grow up and pitch in the big leagues and have a great career."

Mom smiled and mussed my hair. "A million boys have a dream like that, baby. And not one in a million will ever achieve it."

"Maybe so," I said, "but I'm going to be that one in a million, Mom. There are over six hundred players in the majors. About two hundred sixty pitchers. Dad never made it up there, but I will."

"I hope you will," she said. "But, Bobby, it's only a dream, something you want very much when you're young. You don't know what you'll want when you grow up. You might become a doctor or a lawyer. A scientist or a teacher or who knows what? You've got all the time in the world to decide."

"I already decided. I'm going to be a major leaguer."

I got a big hug then and a wet kiss on my cheek. "Whatever you decide," Mom said, "you're going to be great."

She said goodnight and closed the light.

●   ●   ●

It takes about 300 wins to get in the Hall of Fame.

Catfish Hunter made it, and Drysdale, Gibson, Marichal, and Hoyt Wilhelm. Whitey Ford made it with only 284 wins.

And someday, Bobby "Baseball" Ellis will make it, too.

16

Pregame
Warm-up

The day before the Jays game Dad showed up in my room with a catcher's mitt in his hand. "What say you throw me a few?" he said.

"Great."

"Get your glove."

We went out to the driveway. Dad crouched down in front of the garage. "Throw nice and easy," he said, "just get warm."

It felt funny throwing on the flat. I'd gotten used to the feel of the mound on our practice diamond.

I threw nice and easy, like Dad said, and I had great control. "Last one," he called out, and I muscled up and let one fly as fast as I could. It stayed high, like always, and it wasn't very fast. That was me, all right, great control and no swift.

We walked around to the front of the house and

sat down on the porch steps in the sun. "Looking good," Dad said. "How do you feel?"

"Fine."

"Thinking about tomorrow?"

"Some," I lied. I was thinking about it like every two minutes.

"Let's review it," Dad said. "What's the most important thing?"

"Throw strikes."

"Bingo. What else?"

"Keep alert, field my position. Try to plan where I'll throw the ball if it's hit to me."

"Anything else?"

"Hold the runner close. Do my best." I thought for a second or two. "I think that's all."

"One more thing," said Dad. "Stay cool, keep your head. You may walk a few guys, kids may bang you around and score some runs. Just don't let it make you lose your temper. Do your best and stay within yourself, understand?"

I didn't. "What do you mean? I can't jump out of myself."

Dad smiled. "Just do what you can do. You can't take the whole ball team on your shoulders. That's why we call it a team, nine on the field and six on the bench. It's not just you all alone out there against the Jays."

"Okay," I said.

We sat looking at the cars going by on Oak Street, not saying anything.

"Is there something else on your mind?" Dad asked me.

"No."

"Nothing about me yelling at you, maybe?"

I looked Dad in the eyes. "Mom talked to you," I said.

"She didn't have to," said Dad. "I've been thinking about it, all by my lonesome."

"I hate the way you scream at me on the field," I said.

"I know," said Dad. He banged the catcher's mitt against his leg. "I do it for a reason. I want you to be as good as you can be. Maybe too much, I don't know. I'm worried about you. I don't want to see you fail and beat yourself up and get your heart broken."

"I won't fail," I said.

"I still think your natural position is second base," Dad said. "But you want to be a pitcher . . . so here we are."

"I'm gonna be great," I said, hoping that was true.

"Good," said Dad. He gave me a hug and we went into the house.

The rest of the day was an ordinary Saturday. Mom went shopping at the A & P. Dad worked at his desk in the den. Sammy went off to the mall with some friends.

I spent the day being nervous.

I planned on going to bed early because the game started at ten in the morning. I got a couple of books off Dad's shelves and went up to my room right after dinner. They were both pitcher's books: Tom Seaver and Catfish Hunter. I wanted to read about how they did in the first games they pitched.

I was sitting on my bed when Grandpa came in. "How's the star pitcher?" he wanted to know.

"Nervous."

"You're supposed to be," he said. "If you were calm, I'd worry about you. Just zip that old *pelota* right in there tomorrow. You'll do fine."

"Thanks."

Grandpa left and Sammy came in. He rubbed my right arm for luck. "Be strong tomorrow," he said, and left.

Then Mom came and gave me a kiss goodnight. "You're going to strike out about ninety kids and win it," she said.

"The most I can strike out is twenty-one," I said. "It's a seven-inning game."

"You could play extra innings," she said.

"I sure hope not."

"Good luck, darling," she said, closing the light on her way out.

After I got under the covers, Dad came tiptoeing in. He bent down and kissed my cheek. "Good luck tomorrow," he said.

Well, I thought, staring at the ceiling in the dark, I sure have my family on my side. It had been like a parade through my room.

I started pitching in my mind. I was up against an all-star team, and before Reggie Jackson came up, I was asleep.

I got up about six o'clock and it was light out. I took a shower to wake up and get loose, then dressed in my uniform. Downstairs in the kitchen I met Dad and Sammy. Dad was making pancakes, and I had two of them with a glass of milk. Dad and Sammy were talking away to each other, but I mostly said nothing.

I was too busy being scared.

We left for the field really early. I wore my zip

jacket over my uniform because the weather was cloudy and cool. We unloaded all the equipment at diamond number 3, where we were playing, and I helped Sammy set out the bases. Then I sat down on the home-team bench, which was on the first-base side of the field.

Pretty soon kids and their parents started arriving. Some of the Jays came along in their blue-and-white uniforms. Jason showed up with his dad, who went away to sit in the bleachers. Mouth arrived and sat down with Jason and me. We didn't say much, and then when most of the team was there, Sammy led us around the field for a couple of laps. Then he broke out the ball bag, and we started to throw on the sidelines. I just tossed nice and easy, saving my arm for the game.

Bob McCarron was the manager of the Jays, and he came over to talk to Dad for a bit. Dad pointed me out to him, and Mr. McCarron came over to where I was tossing and wished me luck. The Jays took infield practice, and then we followed them and did the same. It seemed to me that everyone was nervous. There wasn't the casual kidding around like at practice, and nobody was yelling or calling out stuff.

Two umpires in blue uniforms showed up, and Dad knew both of them. It was almost game time.

Sammy whistled to me, and I walked down the right-field line with him to get warm. Sammy said to start easy, and then he set up in a crouch with his big mitt. I started tossing with my zip jacket still on, then dropped it when I felt sweat beginning on my back.

Jimmy Rossillo came down the line and took over from Sammy, who stood by, watching. I practiced my stretch move for a few pitches, then threw a few as hard as I could. "One more, one more!" Jimmy yelled, and I let it fly for a strike.

I put my jacket on again, and the three of us walked back to the bench. Dad got us together and gave the whole team a little talk. To tell the truth, I don't remember what he said. I don't think any of us were listening much. Then the umpire pointed at our bench. Dad said, "Starting team," and we ran out on the field. A few cheers and some applause came from parents in the stands.

The plate umpire came walking out to the mound in his clunky steel-tipped shoes. He handed me a brand-new baseball. "Good luck, son," he said. I just nodded at him and began to throw a few tosses to Jimmy behind the plate. On first base, Jason was warming up the infield with easy bouncing grounders. Mike Lum was at third, Tony at short, and Mouth was standing down by second base.

The other umpire came walking out to stand between first and second. The plate umpire looked out at me, raised his right arm, and yelled, "Play ball!"

I stood just off the mound, rubbing up the ball. It felt slick and shiny in my hand, and my mouth was suddenly full of cotton. Outside the batter's box the first Jays batter was taking a few practice swings. I put my glove on my hand and walked up onto the mound. The batter stepped into the box.

Here we go.

17

Bobby Baseball's First Game

I know I'll remember that moment for the rest of my life: the day cool and cloudy, parents sitting in the bleachers behind the low fence, how huge the umpire looked behind Jimmy, the smooth feel of the ball in my hand.

And how scared I was.

My heart was pumping like crazy. I took a couple of big breaths and blew them out slowly, looking at the batter. He was a small, skinny kid, wearing number 12, and his batting helmet covered most of his face.

Sammy and Dad started clapping hands from the bench and Dad yelled, "Let's hear it out there, Hawks!"

I stepped up on the rubber and set my cap down hard on my head. Behind me I heard the chatter begin.

"To me, to me, to me," Jimmy was yelling behind the plate.

"No batter! No batter!" Mike was saying at third base.

"Gaydee gets a gaydee Go!" Tony at short sang.

"Bobby-baby, baby-Bobby!" Mouth screamed in her loud voice.

"Be good, be good, beeeegoood!" Jase chattered at first base.

I wound up and threw the first one wide, but it didn't matter. The Jays' batter swung anyway and missed. He missed the next one, too, which was right down the middle, and then struck out on a ball in the dirt. One up, one down, my first strikeout.

Funny thing, I wasn't nervous anymore. When I got the ball back from Jimmy, I rubbed it and started to feel that everything was going to be all right. I had my confidence back. I felt strong, I was going to be great today.

And that's the way it turned out. Mostly, anyway.

I walked the second batter, we got a groundout to Jase, and the next batter hit one past Mike and the Jays had a run. But the next kid popped up to Tony and we were out of it.

In our half of the first we scored four runs—mostly on walks and errors and one good hit by Jimmy, batting sixth—but that was the start we needed. The game turned out to be easy. We scored in the second, a pair of runs, knocked in when their shortstop threw away Mouth's little dribbler.

Six to one, Hawks. End of two.

When I walked out to the mound for the third, Dad was coming across the diamond from coaching third base. "Rock steady," he said to me, "you're do-ing great."

I walked the leadoffer in the third, Mike messed up a hard-hit ball, but I struck out the next kid—the Jays were overswinging like mad all day. Then there was a groundout, but the Jays cleanup hitter shot a hard single to left, and the Jays had a pair of runs.

We came right back and scored a big five runs. Jase doubled down the line in right, Mike Marder singled, the Jays made two bad errors in a row, and we got three walks before Freddie knocked in two runs with a shot to center.

Hawks, 11—Jays, 3.

On the bench we were jumping up and down and cheering. "Is this fun, or what?" Mouth asked me and everyone. Jason's mouth was full of bubble gum and he stuck it over his front teeth and smiled like a tooth-less maniac.

In the top of the fifth all our subs came into the game. Those were the rules: every player on the roster had to play at least half the game. So Ned took over from Jimmy behind the plate, Jackie replaced Jase at first, and so on. The only ones to stay in the game were Tony at short, Freddie in center, and myself.

It didn't make much difference.

The Jays were terrible. They stunk up so many plays in the field, it was funny. We had a swell time on the bench watching them kick the ball around, shy away from hard-hit grounders, and throw the ball wild all over the place. Dad was right, defense wins ball games. The Jays just gave the game away.

Final score: Hawks, 17—Jays, 8.

Two kids on the Jays hit me hard. The rest swung

at bad pitches, and my fielders took care of them. I struck out seven, the last one to end the game. Ned came out to the mound and the rest of the team followed, and we high-fived and low-tenned and generally behaved like a bunch of happy nuts. Then Dad made us get in a line, and we shook hands with all the Jays who came by. I kept saying, "Nice game," as I shook hands with them, all the while thinking, "Yeah, nice game for us, horrible game for you."

Whether you win or lose, you still have to make sure you go home with all the equipment you brought to the field. I helped Sammy round up the bases and fill the duffel bags with our bats, batting helmets, catcher's gear, and the balls used in the game.

"Nice game," Dad said to me and rubbed my arm. Mom and Grandpa had come onto the field from the stands by then. Mom turned my cap around and kissed my forehead, and Grandpa gave me a high five. "Major league," he said to me.

They went off home in Mom's car while we loaded the wagon. I sat up front with Dad, and Sammy sat in the back. Sammy was looking at the scorebook he had on his lap. "Know how many strikeouts you had?" he asked me.

"Seven."

Sammy smiled. "I knew you were keeping count."

"And I walked six—"

"Too many," said Dad.

"But I gave up only about five hits," I said.

Sammy whooped from behind me. "*Ten* hits," he said, "that's the way I scored it."

"No way," I insisted, turning around to look at

Sammy. "Those were errors, not hits. Mouth messed up two, Tony and Mike and KP, too."

"Get real," said Sammy, "those were hits, pal."

"Some official scorer you are," I said.

"Hits," Sammy said, making a face at me.

"You did okay," Dad said, squeezing my knee with his big hand. "But let's face it, the Jays were awful. Bob McCarron told me before the game that the Jays weren't ready, and he was right. So it's hard to tell how good the Hawks are yet. I think our defense was pretty good, but we didn't hit all that much."

"We got thirteen hits," Sammy said.

"About half of them should have been caught," Dad said. "So I wouldn't get all puffed up yet. We'll see how good we are when we play the Bankers and the Rangers. Jack Sheridan always has a good team."

"I don't care about that," I said. "I feel puffed up."

Dad smiled. "So you should. For the first time out, you did all right, Bob-o."

For the rest of the day I kept replaying the game in my head, thinking a lot about those third and fourth Jays batters who kept hitting everything I threw up to the plate.

After dinner I wandered into Sammy's room. He was entering the stats of the game into his computer. Sammy has a program in there that produces box scores of games. When he put the finished box of the game up on the screen, it looked terrific. "Make one of those for me," I asked him, so Sammy printed it out.

I took the box score to my room and read it for a while. I went 0 for 5 at the plate, so my batting average was a big zero. I tried to figure out my ERA, but I didn't know what to do because I only pitched seven innings, not nine. It wouldn't be too great anyway, that I knew.

I got out my thick black marker and put the date on the box score. Then I wrote in big letters, BOBBY BASEBALL'S FIRST WIN! and stuck it in my baseball book.

The future Hall of Famer's first lifetime victory, baseball fans. Bobby "Baseball" Ellis—number 9 in your souvenir program and number 1 in your hearts.

HAWKS, 17—JAYS, 8

JAYS	ab	r	h	bi		HAWKS	ab	r	h	bi
Rosman cf	4	1	1	0		Alston rf	3	3	2	1
Hayes ss, p	4	1	1	0		Gomez ss	4	2	1	1
Westberg 3b	3	2	3	3		Lum 3b	2	3	1	1
Olding 2b	3	2	3	2		Marder lf	2	1	1	2
Shepherd c	2	0	0	0		Miller cf	4	2	3	4
Schmalz 1b	2	0	1	0		Rossillo c	2	0	2	2
Powell rf	3	1	0	0		Moss 1b	2	1	1	0
Moreno lf,p	2	0	0	0		DeMuth 2b	1	2	1	0
Medney p,lf	4	1	0	0		Ellis p	5	0	0	0
Tenney lf	2	0	1	1		Peters 2b	2	1	1	1
Grose rf	2	0	0	0		Robbins c	2	1	0	0
Black c	2	0	0	0		Tucker 3b	2	1	0	0
Asher 3b	1	0	0	0		Ulman 1b	2	0	0	0
Langer ss	1	0	0	0		Gardner lf	2	0	0	0
Kaufman 2b	1	0	0	0		Moriarty rf	1	0	0	0
Totals	36	8	10	6			36	17	13	12

JAYS	102	201	2 — — 8
HAWKS	425	222	X — — 17

E— ROSMAN, HAYES 2, OLDING 2, GROSE 2, ASHER, LANGER; LUM, GOMEZ, DEMUTH, PETERS 2, MORIARTY. DP— JAYS 1. 2B— HAYES, OLDING, SCHMALZ; GOMEZ, ROSSILLO 2, MOSS, PETERS. SB— WESTBERG, OLDING, POWELL 2; GOMEZ, LUM 2, MILLER, ROSSILLO, DEMUTH 2. SF— PETERS. LOB— JAYS 12, HAWKS 14.

JAYS	IP	H	R	ER	BB	SO
Medney, L 0–1	3	6	11	6	5	4
Moreno	2	5	4	2	3	1
Hayes	1	2	2	1	2	2

HAWKS						
Ellis, W 1–0	7	10	8	5	6	7

Umpires: Home, Rodney; Bases, DeGroot

18

"Hawks Rule!"

The way Dad treated us at practice the week after the Jays game you might have thought we'd lost instead of won.

"You people didn't play nearly as well as you can," he told us. And he ran us ragged all afternoon. It was defense first, of course, but Dad was worried about our not hitting, too.

We got lots of batting practice. Freddie threw most of it, with Mike and me helping out. Freddie was looking better on the mound. And you could see he had the hang of fielding the position now.

Mouth was becoming a really good bunter. She was small to begin with, sort of low to the ground, and she got the idea of cradling the bat and just dumping the ball along the third-base line. She could run pretty well for a girl. No, let me be honest—Mouth ran faster than most kids on the team, boy or girl.

Dad spent a lot of time with her. He liked Mouth a lot. "Way to lay it down!" he'd yell when she bunted a good one. By the end of the week Dad decided to bat Mouth in the leadoff spot. "Bunt like that and there's no way you get thrown out," he told her. "And you're so small, you'll get a lot of walks, too."

After our last practice that week we gave a lift home to Mouth, Nancy, and Jase. Mouth didn't stop talking the whole way home. "Those Lions are dead meat," she said. "We're gonna murder 'em."

"Let's hope so," Dad said.

"No contest," she said. "Hawks rule!"

"All right!" said Jason. "Hawks rule!"

"Hawks rule!" Nancy chipped in, and so did I.

And that was the beginning of that saying, which became a chant of the team. "Hawks rule!" was something we began to say when someone got a hit or made a good play. And if you scored a run and came back to the bench, you did a high five with everyone and we all yelled, "Hawks rule!"

I felt great the morning of the game with the Lions. I was looking forward to pitching and playing ball.

The weather came up beautiful, sunny and warm. As warm as the day was, the Hawks were even hotter.

We creamed the Lions, we murdered them, we slaughtered them, we slugged them, ripped them up, wiped them out . . . and we beat them, too.

Final score: Hawks, 16—Lions, 7.

It isn't hard to win when the opposing pitcher walks the first five batters on your team, the fielders behind him make three errors, we get a couple of timely hits, and score a big eight runs in the top of the first inning. That is one terrific way to start a ball game.

The kid who pitched for the Lions was gone before the first inning was over. And the kid who replaced him wasn't too good either. We hit pretty well. Jase had two hits, Tony a pair of doubles, Jimmy knocked in four runs, and Freddie had three extra-base hits. Mouth scored four runs in four times at bat, walking three times and bunting her way on once.

I even got one hit myself, except that Sammy called it an error on the shortstop.

You would think that if your very own big brother is the official scorer, he would try to help out your batting average instead of hurting it. But that's the way Sammy is. I think he takes after Dad. You have to do something great—like get a genuine hit—to get any credit.

I pitched okay, just like last time. I put the ball over the plate and they couldn't hit it.

Well, some of them could hit it.

They had ten hits, but I walked only three. And we only made three errors. I struck out six, to go with my seven the game before.

Two games, two wins. Fourteen innings pitched, thirteen strikeouts. And another terrific box score to go in my memory book.

When the game was finally over, we shook hands with all the Lions. Jerry Wexler, the Lions' manager, came over and shook my hand. Then he turned to Dad. "Sorry we didn't give you more of a tussle, Chuck," he said.

"Well," said Dad, "that's about as good as we can play."

"You've got a nice team," said Mr. Wexler. "I figure it's between you, the Bankers, and the Rangers this year. Jack Sheridan's crew is crackerjack, I hear."

We packed up our gear and got into the station wagon. Nan, Jase, and Mouth squeezed into the backseat with me. We kept crowing, "Hawks rule!" on the way home until Dad complained we were making him dizzy.

At dinner I kept blabbing away about the game, telling Mom and Grandpa what happened because they hadn't come to see us play. "We may never lose," I told Mom between bites.

"Highly unlikely," she said.

"It could happen," I said. "We might be the best team in the league. And I might be the best pitcher."

"And if you had wings, you could fly," Sammy said.

I tried to kick him under the table and missed. "Has there ever been a team in the Mustang League that won every game?" I asked Dad.

"I don't think so," he said.

"That's just what the Hawks are going to do," I said.

"Now, Bob," he said, "just simmer down. We haven't played the really good teams yet. The Bankers and the Rangers are two and zero, like us. They may be better than we are."

"No way," I said. "We're going to sweep. And I am going to have an undefeated season. I don't think any team can beat me."

"Don't build yourself up too much, young man," Dad said.

"Exactly right," Grandpa agreed. "Remember, Bob, pride often goeth before a fall."

I heard Grandpa say that, but I didn't know exactly what he meant. "It's not the fall," I said, "it's only the spring. And the Hawks are on a winning streak."

"Winning streak?" Sammy grinned at me. "Two games? That's a winning streak?"

"You'll see," I said. "We're going all the way to the top."

Of course, I had no way of knowing what was going to happen to me and the team. Or how that dumb remark was going to come back and haunt me.

19

Winning Streak

I was having another great day, or the Tigers were as awful as the Jays and the Lions. You could look at it either way.

We were ahead, 11 to 3, as we batted in the top of the sixth inning. Then Jimmy doubled, Jase singled him home, and we were ahead by nine runs.

Dad whistled from where he was coaching at third base, and Sammy ran out to take his place. Dad jogged in to the bench and called Freddie and me over to him. "How do you feel, Freddie?" Dad asked him.

Freddie shrugged in his usual way.

"Think you can pitch a few innings for us?" Dad asked.

"Hey," I said, "I'm pitching great! You can't take me out!"

Dad turned to me and gave me one of his laser

looks. "Sit down on the bench, Bobby," he said. "Freddie, you get Ned to warm you up."

Freddie ran off down the line with Ned, and I grabbed Dad's arm. "What are you doing?" I yelled at him. "I want to finish the game."

Dad shook off my hand. He looked as mad as I've ever seen him.

"Back to the bench," he said in a kind of low growl.

"It's stupid!"

"SIT DOWN!" Dad shouted back at me, then he turned and ran back out to coach third base again.

I whirled away and kicked at the dirt. I was boiling mad and I didn't care who knew it. I took off my cap and threw it to the bench, then picked up my glove and whomped it to the ground. I kicked the bench.

"Don't break your foot," Jase said.

I kicked the bench again.

"Or the bench," Jase added.

"Just shut up!" I yelled at him and sat down hard on the bench. I put my head down and stared at the ground. I know myself and I know my temper.

I was just on the edge of losing control.

I started to count slowly in my head. By the time I reached fifty, the inning was over.

The teams changed sides, and Dad came back to the bench. I tried to catch his eye, but he wouldn't look at me and went way down to the other end of the bench to sit down.

Sammy and his scorebook settled down beside me. "Keep it under control," he said to me.

"Oh, yeah?" I said. "Why?"

"So you don't make any more of a fool of yourself than you already have," said Sammy.

"Why is he doing this?" I asked Sammy. "I was doing good."

"We're way ahead," Sammy said. "Dad's giving Freddie some experience out there, that's all."

"He's gonna blow the game," I said.

"We're up by nine runs," said Sammy. "Relax."

"But it's my ball game," I said. "That's my third win out there."

Sammy stared at me through his eyeglasses. "That's funny," he said, "I thought the name of this team was the Hawks, not the Bobbys."

I shut up and watched the game. What I saw was Freddie walking the first batter and then wild-pitching him to second base. He looked really scared out on the mound.

Freddie has a great arm. Even I have to admit that. But if you can't put the ball over the plate, it doesn't matter if you can throw as hard as Superman.

Fred walked the next batter, a kid I'd struck out twice. Dad called time and went running out to the mound. I knew exactly what Dad was saying to Fred out there, because I'd heard it myself. Settle down, Dad was saying, throw strikes.

No sooner had Dad come back to the bench than Freddie tried to pick off the runner at second base and threw the ball into center field. By the time we got the ball, a run had scored. The next man hit a ground ball and another run crossed the plate.

Now we only had a seven-run lead.

Then Freddie walked another kid on four pitches.

The whole bench was pretty quiet. Ned called time

and slowly walked out to the mound. He talked to Freddie until the plate umpire came back out to break it up. It seemed to take a week for Ned to get back behind the plate, put his mask on, and get set.

Dad was on his feet, clapping his hands. "You're the man, Freddie! You're the man!"

Maybe the time Ned took helped Freddie settle down. He began to find the plate much better, and the ball started to pop into Ned's mitt. Fred put the side down without any more runs. The lead was still seven.

Fred came to the bench, and Dad made a place for him to sit down. I saw Dad give Fred a hug and I looked away.

I shouldn't have worried about losing a win. Fred was looking good out on the mound now. We scored some more, and the game was never in doubt again. Not the way Fred was throwing. In the seventh inning he struck out the side to end the game.

I'd pitched five innings in all, giving up six hits, three walks, and I'd struck out four. It was my third win in a row.

Why did I feel so terrible when the game was over?

20

Five-Hundred-Pound Gorilla, II

It was a loud and happy ride back home in the station wagon. For some people.

Mouth never stopped talking, and Nan couldn't quit giggling. Jason kept singing his Savage Towels song. But Dad didn't say a word and neither did I.

We dropped off Mouth and Nan and then Jason. Dad pulled the wagon all the way up the drive near the garage.

I helped Sammy unload the equipment and stash it away. Dad came around the wagon and waited by the garage door. "Sammy," he said, "you go on in the house. I want to have a word with Bobby."

Sammy gave me a look and then walked away. The next minute Dad was in my face. "I want to hear an apology," he said, "this very minute."

"What for?" I said, which was pretty dumb. I knew that I'd acted like a baby.

Dad put a hand up and started ticking things off on his fingers. "You acted like a spoiled brat, for one. You tossed your cap. You threw your glove. You kicked the bench. You yelled at me on the field in front of your teammates." He gave me a hard look. "You want more?"

"No."

"Players don't yell at managers," Dad said. "Not in Mustang League or any league. I can't have that. And if you were anyone else but my son, I'd bench you right here and now."

"No," I said, "please don't bench me. I was doing so good and then you pulled me out of the game."

Dad folded his arms across his chest. "It doesn't matter what I did. It's what *you* did. You disobeyed me in front of our whole team, the Tigers, the umpires, the people in the stands. That can't happen again. I won't permit it, do you understand?"

"Yes."

"Remember when I agreed to let you be on the team, I told you what a manager is? Do you remember?"

"Yeah," I said, "a five-hundred-pound gorilla."

Dad nodded. "I'm still waiting for an apology."

I took a breath and said, "Okay, I'm sorry I lost my head. I apologize."

"And I'll never do it again," said Dad.

I couldn't look in his eyes. "Okay, okay," I said. "And I'll never do it again."

"You better not do it again," he said. "Because if you do, you'll get blisters on your butt from sitting on the bench so long. Do you hear me?"

"I hear you," I said.

We stood side by side for a minute that way, me not looking at him. I was waiting for something, a hand on my head, a squeeze or a pat, but Dad's arms remained folded across his chest.

"I hated when you took me out of the game," I said. "Why'd you do it? I was rolling along, I could've kept going."

"I did it for the team," Dad said. "A team needs more than one pitcher. And Freddie needed the chance."

"What about me?" I said, my voice rising a little. "I could have had a complete game. I could have got more strikeouts. I could have finished the game as good as Freddie did."

Dad sighed and shook his head. "Bobby, Bobby," he said. "That's three *I'* s in a row. But baseball isn't about *I'* s, it's about *us*. Us is a team. Nine people. Not just a pitcher looking for personal glory. You play for the team, Bobby, not the record books."

"Would you take me out if I struck out twenty-one guys?"

"That's another *I,* isn't it?" Dad said.

"How about if I pitched a no-hitter? That would help the team, you know it would."

Dad started shutting the garage door, pulling it down and letting the lock slide into place. "How can a kid be so smart and act so dumb?" he asked. "You still don't get it, do you? You're still wrapped up in your records, aren't you?"

I didn't know what to say.

That's when Dad turned and started walking toward the back door.

I let him go inside the house before I followed.

We didn't talk about what happened at dinner. Dad didn't say anything about me acting up on the field, and I sure didn't want to bring it up.

I kept away from Dad. I knew he was mad at me. And I wasn't feeling so lovey-dovey toward him, either.

That night I went into Sammy's room and asked him to make me a box score.

"I already did," he said, handing it over. He pushed his glasses on top of his head and rubbed his eyes. "You're benched, right?"

"Nope," I said.

Sammy's eyes widened in surprise. "No? Why not?"

I shrugged.

"You're not benched," Sammy said, "I can't believe it. For sure Dad wouldn't've let me get away with what you pulled."

"Maybe it's because we play the Bankers next. He needs me."

"Don't be stupid," Sammy said. "Dad doesn't think like that. He'd bench his mother if she looked at him cross-eyed. He's giving you another chance, that must be it."

"And I deserve it," I said. "He shouldn't've pulled me out of the game, and he knows it."

"So dumb!" Sammy said, clapping his hand to his head. "You are too dumb to breathe, kid."

"Did I win three games or not?"

"Oh, my dopey, dreamy brother," Sammy said. "I forgot. You are Bobby Baseball, who's never going to lose a game. You're going to the Hall of Fame, right from Mustang League. Move over, Sandy Koufax, here comes Bobby."

"Have you been looking in my Baseball Book?" I said. "That's private, Sammy, you keep your hands off it, you hear?"

"I wouldn't touch your stupid book," Sammy said. "Will you wake up, you crazy kid! You can't pitch and you still don't know it. Can't throw hard enough to break a storm window from ten feet. And if kids didn't swing at that nothing sinker you've got, you'd never get anyone out."

I knew Sammy was just trying to get me mad, but I wouldn't let him. "Three wins, no losses, Sam. Seventeen strikeouts in nineteen innings. Are you jealous?"

"Of you? A silly kid who walks around dreaming he's the greatest thing since sliced bread? If you ever got a foul tip on your foot, you'd run home crying to Mom. You're such a baby."

"Oh, yeah? If I'm such a baby, why are you so mad?"

"You know why," Sammy said. "Because Dad's treating you much better than he ever did me. You don't know how lucky you are, dummy. Now get out of here and let me do my work." With that, Sammy pulled his glasses down and swiveled his chair away from me.

I took my box score and left.

● ● ●

Why is everyone so mad at me?

I want to be the best. I want to win ball games, same as Dad does.

I want to strike out a zillion batters and get my name in the record books.

What's wrong with that?

I'm a better pitcher than Freddie Miller any day!

21

Wrong Pitch

Sunday afternoon we worked on getting the lawn in shape. It's one of the jobs around the house I really like. Sammy and me did most of the raking. We use these grass rakes made of bamboo. The idea is to get up the brown grass that grows over the winter and leave the good grass alone.

The brown grass is what Dad calls thatch. It's really old dead grass that turns brown in the cold and snow. It takes a long time to get up all the thatch from in front of our house and down the driveway and in the backyard.

We took a break when we finished it all, sitting on the old wooden bench under the apple tree in the backyard. The day was warm and sunny, a beauty. Mom brought out some iced tea and we drank it while Grandpa walked around and inspected the work we'd done.

He pointed out a few spots we'd missed and then sat down with us. "I can't wait for the first mowing," he said. "That smell of cut grass is what summer's all about, boys."

"We've got a while till it gets cut," said Dad. "We're behind. Should have reseeded a couple weeks ago."

Sammy went off to rake the spots Grandpa had pointed out while Dad got the grass seed out of the garage. I raked up the bare spots of ground for him, and Dad tossed down the seed. In a week or so those bare earth spots will begin to have little shoots of grass growing on them. I love the way they look. It always makes me think the lawn is growing a new green beard.

At the end of Friday's practice Dad got us together and we sat down by the fence behind third base. "Just a few words about our next two games," he said. "The Bankers this weekend and the Rangers next week."

"Hawks rule!" Mouth yelled.

Dad grinned at her. "I sure hope so, Mouth. But don't be upset if we don't win. The Bankers and the Rangers are the top teams. They won't give us easy runs or hand over the games, the way it's been happening so far. If we fall behind, don't panic. The important thing is to play as well as we can. Okay, Hawks?"

"Okay!" we yelled back.

We had a later starting time for the Bankers game —2:00 P.M. So I slept late and had breakfast in my pj's and robe. Then I kept busy in my room until it was time to get into my uniform.

Grandpa came by to wish me luck. He and Mom

were staying home again. "You just keep that old potato humming," he said. "Fog it right in there."

"I will."

"That's the ticket." Grandpa gave my arm one final rub for luck and then went off to take a nap.

Jase came along to get a ride, then we loaded our stuff and took off for Schenley Park.

The Bankers were taking infield practice in their green-and-gold uniforms. They didn't look any bigger or stronger than us.

I watched them while I tossed easy on the side with Jase and Mouth, then we sat down on the bench. "Let's beat these guys," I said.

"Oh, okay," said Jase, like it was a new idea. "You know they're three and zero, just like us. And they can hit."

"No problem," I said.

"These guys are nothing," Mouth said. "Bobby Baseball is gonna shut them out."

"Good," said Jase. "I'm glad that's taken care of."

I felt great when I warmed up with Jimmy, nice and loose. I muscled up a few times to try to make Jimmy's mitt pop, like Freddie did, but I only managed to do it once. I quit after that, came back to the bench, and wiped the sweat off with a towel. Dad came over to give Jimmy and me some last-minute words. "These guys can hit," he said. "Keep the ball down and just play your game."

I warmed up on the mound when it was time. I was in no hurry. I held the ball a moment, rubbing it, looking around. There was a big crowd for the game, lots of parents in the bleachers. I heard our infield chatter behind me and the rest of our team on the bench.

I wound up and threw my first pitch, and the batter hit it for a clean double to left.

One pitch, one hit.

Mouth ran the ball in from second and placed it in my glove. "Lucky hit, Bobby-baby. Let's get 'em."

I got ahead of the next batter, and then he singled through the shortstop hole, scoring the runner from second. Two batters and we were behind already.

I threw another pitch. Whack! Double to right.

"What in the world here?" I asked myself. This should not be happening. I wasn't mad or scared. I just didn't understand it.

I worked carefully to their cleanup batter, a big kid with lots of muscles, and finally walked him. Two on, one run in, nobody out.

From behind me I heard Mouth call time and she came running over to the mound. "Bobby-baby, what's up?" she asked.

"You tell me."

"Forget it," she said, "bear down. We need a strikeout, okay?"

Okay, I thought, fastball to the max. The trouble was I couldn't throw strikes that way—the ball stayed up—and I walked the batter to load the bases.

Now Dad called time and he came jogging out to the mound with Jimmy. "You're overthrowing," he said. "Throw strikes and let's get some outs."

"Right," I said.

The next Banker hit a shot over Jase's head at first that rolled all the way to the fence. Triple, three more runs across. Bankers had four runs, and there was still no one out.

I was getting shelled and I couldn't understand why. I wasn't doing anything different. I was throwing like I had in our first three games.

Keep the ball down, I told myself. Luckily I got a ground ball out, Mouth to Jason. I was happy to get it, even though the fifth Banker run scored.

The next Banker hit one right back to me on one hop. I threw him out with no trouble.

One more out, please!

The next kid hit a solid line drive right into Tony's glove at short. One foot right or left and it would have been a hit.

I ran to the bench in a kind of daze. I was throwing my best, and they were hitting it like batting practice.

"Okay, okay!" Dad was saying, clapping his hands. "We come right back. Let's go!" Then he ran out to coach third.

The Hawks went down one-two-three.

I walked out to the mound and met Dad halfway. "Rock steady," he said to me.

"I am."

"Right."

Okay, Bobby Baseball, I said to myself as I warmed up. You've got to forget about being five runs behind. Just make believe the game starts right here.

It worked for the first batter, the opposing pitcher. He hit a roller to Jason, and I ran over to cover first base like I was supposed to, and he was out easy as I stepped on the bag.

"Kazooty," Jase said. "One down."

Now the top of the Banker batting order was up again. I took a deep breath and toed the rubber.

Whack! Single to right.

Bonk! Single to center.

Konk! Double to left, scoring a run.

I'd seen this last inning. It was like an instant replay. I was so mad I couldn't even spit.

Jimmy came walking out toward the mound, his mask in his hand, and when I looked over my shoulder, there was Dad coming out too.

"Ball," he said, sticking out his hand for it.

"One more batter," I said.

"Ball."

"I'm not even warmed up yet."

"It's not your day," said Dad, "ball."

"I'll strike this guy out . . ."

"Give me the ball."

"Come on," I said. "Oh, Dad, please!"

"Give me the ball!" Dad said, gritting his teeth.

"NO!" I yelled, exploding right there and then. I took two running steps toward home plate, my arm went back, and I threw that baseball toward home as high and as hard as I could.

It was an amazing moment.

If I hadn't been blood-boiling mad, maybe I'd remember more of it.

But I do remember the ball sailing up and up over the backstop . . . the umpire at home looking up in shock as the ball sailed so high over his head . . . the way the people in the stands shut up, then began yelling and clapping and laughing . . . the ball flying onto the diamond behind ours and rolling across the infield there . . . and the groan that came from Dad.

The ump pointed out at me and raised up his arm and thumb. I was out of the game, but I knew that.

I felt a strong hand grab my shoulder. *"Get on the bench and get out of my sight,"* said Dad in a hard voice.

When I looked at him, his face was red under his baseball cap.

I began walking to the bench. People in the stands were laughing at me. My teammates on the bench looked scared of me, like I was going to start attacking them. The way I was feeling, maybe I would if anyone said one word to me. I was mad enough to smash the bench with a bat. No, make that mad enough to *eat* the bench without salt and pepper.

I sat down, pulled my cap down low, and put my hands together so I wouldn't punch anyone. One thing I knew I wouldn't do.

No way I was going to start crying.

22

Guilty, Your Honor

In case you're thinking the Hawks started hitting and we won it in the last inning with a home run, forget it.

We lost the game, all right. Ten to three, if you really have to know.

Freddie came in and pitched pretty good. He only gave them three runs on his own, after I messed up everything completely. Not that I was seeing anything too plainly after my temper boiled over.

Only Jason and Mouth came to sit near me during the game. For the rest of my teammates, it was like I had some rare and mysterious disease that was catching. They kept away from me.

I remember Jason telling me that if I'd thrown pitches like I threw that ball over the backstop, I'd still be out there.

I didn't think it was funny at the time.

Mouth said, "You sure get mad, don't you?"

I didn't answer her. Or anybody else the whole afternoon.

It was not a happy car ride home. Even Mouth was quiet, for once. I helped Sammy and Dad put our equipment away in the garage. Before we went in the house, Dad stopped me. "After dinner, in the den. We'll have a talk."

"Okay." I nodded, although I really wanted to get it over with right then and there.

I kissed Mom, who was waiting, and told her we'd lost. I didn't tell her anything else. If you want the truth, I felt terrible. Waiting to talk to Dad was scary. Like when you know you messed up a test in school and you have to wait till the next day to get it back.

I went upstairs and took a shower. I let the hot water spray on my back and my head and tried not to think too much.

But I just couldn't get my mind off what I'd done. I kept seeing that ball sailing high and far over the backstop. I kept hearing Dad's angry voice again.

Why had I done that?

It was about as bad as you could act on a ball field without actually hitting the umpire.

I'd seen players get mad when I watched games on TV. Some yelled at umpires, kicked the dirt, or threw a bat down when they struck out. I even remember seeing one pitcher throw his glove into the dugout when he got knocked out of a game.

But I can't remember seeing a pitcher throw a ball over the backstop when his manager came to take him out. Not ever.

I got dressed again and sat in my room, waiting for dinner to be ready. There was a ball game on TV, but I didn't care about it. My stomach was hurting. And not because I was hungry.

I was ashamed of myself. That was the truth of it.

Every bad thing you can say about a kid came into my mind. *He's a spoiled brat.* Yep, that was me. *He can't control himself.* Guilty, your honor. *He throws temper tantrums.* And baseballs over backstops.

Why had I done that? I kept asking myself that question over and over. But I couldn't face the answer.

It was dinnertime and I went downstairs to the table. By the way Mom looked at me, I knew Dad had told her all about what happened. I was hoping no one would mention it. I don't think I could have sat there and discussed my behavior in front of the family.

I didn't eat much, either. It was hard to swallow anything when I couldn't look Dad in the eye across the table. Luckily Grandpa got started on one of his made-up stories. It was about a man who had a pig that was so smart he let it live in his house. It got everybody else laughing and talking, which was fine with me. I only listened and picked at my dinner.

I helped Sammy clear the table after Mom and Dad had their coffee. Then Dad gave me a nod with his head, and I followed him into the den.

He sat down in the chair behind his desk and looked at me.

"I apologize," I said before he could get started. "I'm really sorry for what I did. I lost my temper and acted bad and I want you to know I'll never do it again."

Dad frowned. "Not good enough," he said, tipping back in his chair, "although it's a start."

"I know I'm benched," I said.

"Oh, yes indeed, you're benched," he said. "And right now I'm thinking about trading you to another team. I'll have to see who has an opening."

My stomach dropped down to my shoes and bounced back up again.

"No, please!" I said, "Please don't do that!"

Dad thought for a second. "Can you give me one good reason why I shouldn't trade you? Do you think there's a manager anywhere who would put up with a player disobeying him like you did? Or could take being so embarrassed by a player? In front of umpires who are friends? And the opposing manager? And to have them know that the player who acted so outrageously is my own son?"

"I'll be good," I pleaded. "I won't do it again, Dad. I promise anything that I won't do it again."

"You won't get the chance to do it again. You are going to sit on the bench until your butt hurts. You are going to sit until you learn how kids should behave on a ball field."

I swallowed hard.

"What got into you?" he asked me.

I shrugged.

"Is that the way you take losing? I really want to know, Bobby. What made you do it?"

I started to speak, but a squeak came out. I swallowed again.

"I just . . . I don't know. It wasn't supposed to be like that."

"Like what?"

"Like what happened. I'm better than that. I'm a great pitcher. I won three games so easy. And then . . ."

"Bobby," said Dad, his voice gentler than before, "you are not a great pitcher."

"I am, too," I said.

"You don't have the arm for it," Dad said, "and now we know you don't have the temperament for it. Forget pitching."

"No," I said, "you're wrong."

"Listen to me," Dad said. "There are some things no coach in the world can teach a player if he doesn't have the talent for it. I can't make a kid run faster. Either you are born to run fast or you're not. And Bobby, I can't help a kid with a weak arm throw like a kid with a strong one.

"You don't have the arm to be a good pitcher, Bob. I knew that from the start. But I gave you a chance, my mistake. You're not a natural. Freddie is. He's got a strong and lively arm."

"I'm as good as Freddie any day," I said.

"No, Bobby, you're not. When you play for me again, you're going to be an infielder. A sub infielder, you understand? Probably I'll have you back up Mouth. If I decide you can play at all."

"But I want to pitch," I said. "I have to."

"No more pitching, get that straight. I'm not going to give in this time. I shouldn't have let you pitch in the first place."

"I pitch or I don't play!" I said really loud. I felt my temper coming up again. My dream of being a great pitcher was on the line.

"You won't pitch, and keep your voice down."

I jumped up from my chair. "Then I quit!" I shouted, and I ran out of the room.

23

Lack of Looseness

What do you do when you think your dad is wrong?

I'll tell you what I did, I kept away from him. And I didn't talk to him. All day Sunday and into Monday.

Oh, I was polite enough. When he asked me to pass the milk, I did. If he asked me a question, I answered him. But I didn't say anything to him on my own.

I was a great pitcher. I wasn't going to stop believing that for all the dads in China.

Sunday afternoon, when Dad and Grandpa were downstairs watching a ball game, I stayed up in my room and wrote in my Baseball Book. I kept the door closed too.

● ● ●

Time to Quit
a story by Bobby "Baseball" Ellis

Big Jack was getting hammered, no doubt
about it. Five runs were in and the bases
were loaded. Over his shoulder, Jack saw
Sparky on the way to the mound.

Slug McGurk came out from behind the
plate and beat Sparky to the mound. "Not
your day, Jack," he said.

"Ball," said Sparky when he got there.

"One more batter," said Jack.

"Ball," said Sparky, sticking out his hand.

Jack handed it over. The relief pitcher was
walking in from the bullpen.

"Take infield practice tomorrow," Sparky
said to Jack.

"What?" Jack wasn't sure he'd heard right.
"Hey," he said, "I'm a pitcher. I'm a great
pitcher."

"Not any more," said Sparky. "I'll play
you somewhere, sometime. Infield, maybe,
as a sub."

**"Oh, no you won't!" Jack yelled on the
mound in front of fifty thousand people,
the umpires, and all of Sparky's friends. "I
QUIT!" Jack yelled, and threw his glove
in the air.**

**When it came down, it hit Sparky in
the head.**

● ● ●

I was ready when Mom came in to kiss me goodnight.

"I already made up my mind, so you don't have to
talk about it," I said. "He's my dad, but I don't have to
play for him."

"No," said Mom, "you don't. And it's okay to be
angry with him right now. But I want you to make up
with him, okay?"

"I will," I said. "Maybe in a year or so."

Mom looked at me. "There's a lot of bulldog in
you," she said.

"I have to keep pitching."

She kissed me, then said, "This, too, shall pass,"
and went out.

I didn't sleep too good that Sunday night. Not because it was Sunday night and there was school the
next day. I kept replaying that Bankers game in my
head.

Pitch—whack!

Pitch—crack!

It's a wonder I did any sleeping at all.

There was something bothering me, and I couldn't

figure it out. If I was so great, why did I get smacked around by the Bankers? If I was such a terrible pitcher, how come I won three games? Like Sammy would say, "It doesn't compute."

I didn't tell anyone in school about quitting the team. They'd find out about it soon enough.

School was the usual, some good, some bad. I couldn't keep my mind from running away with me. I kept seeing myself standing on the mound while base hits whistled past my ears.

I walked home with Jase, not saying much. He was humming some new song by Savage Towels, not "Kalarooty," thank goodness. I was sick of that song.

We went into his house and had milk and cookies. Jase had a wooden mixing spoon in his hand and he swung it like a bat.

I just watched him.

"We're gonna kill those Rangers this Saturday," he said. "And I'm going to hit about three home runs."

"No, you won't," I said.

Jase took another big swing. "You're pretty crabby today," he said.

"I am not."

"Yes, you are. Extremely crabby."

"You keep talking about home runs," I said. "So far you haven't even hit one."

"That's right, but I will."

"Sure you will," I said like I didn't believe it. "You still strike out too much."

"This is true," said Jase, "but I'm working on it."

"You should. There's a lot of room for improvement."

Jase stuck the mixing spoon in his mouth like it was a cigar.

"What's got into you?" he asked.

"Nothing."

"Then why are you being such a grouch?"

"I am *not* a grouch."

"Yes, you are. You've been a grouch all day. Are you worried about the Ranger game?"

"The Ranger game?" I said, my voice rising. "Who cares about the Ranger game? It's not life or death, you know. It's only another stupid ball game in the history of the world."

Jase grinned at me. "You *are* worried about it."

"I am not!"

"Loosen up," Jase said. "There's one thing you've got too much of, Bobby—lack of looseness."

"I'm loose."

"No, you're not. You're about as tight as wet underwear."

"And you," I said, pointing my finger at Jase, "you're so loose, you never worry about anything."

"I worry sometimes," he said.

"Tell me one thing you worry about."

"Savage Towels," he said. "I worry they'll stop making records."

"Don't you worry about making errors?"

"Nope."

"About striking out too much?"

"Nope."

"Don't you ever worry that maybe Jumpin' Jason Moss isn't as hot as he thinks he is?"

"Of course not. Hey, I'm the best."

"Better wake up," I said, "you're a *B* player, like

me. There are lots of kids better than you, and you know it."

"What's a *B* player?"

"An average, ordinary, not-too-good ballplayer, like you and me."

Jase pointed the spoon at me like a gun. "You *are* crabby today."

"What I am is honest. I don't try to fool myself like someone I could name. Like someone in this kitchen."

"Lack of looseness," Jase said. "Totally."

"And my underwear is dry, for your information."

Jase took another cookie and stuck it in his mouth. He chewed and looked at me, then swallowed. "Why are you so mad? And weird?"

I didn't have an answer. We just stared at each other. I know it takes a lot to get Jason mad, which is why we've never fought too much. But I think he was really close to it now.

"Maybe I should go home," I said.

"Maybe."

I got my knapsack and stood up. "I'll see you," I said.

"Right," said Jase.

And I went home without saying anything more.

24

The Grand Old Game

I went up to my room after school on Tuesday and I stayed there.

I looked through my window and saw Dad and Sammy loading the practice gear in the wagon down in the driveway. But I wasn't going with them.

I'd quit the team and I was going to stay quit.

Sammy came running upstairs and stuck his head in my doorway. "Are you coming, or not? Dad wants to know."

"No," I said.

"You're sure about that?" he asked.

"Yes."

"Last chance," Sammy said.

"Have a good practice."

Sammy shook his head. "Then good-bye, sucker."

I heard Sammy run down the stairs, heard the back door slam behind him. Then I watched from my

window as the station wagon backed out of the driveway and pulled away down the street.

I couldn't concentrate on my homework, so I gave
it up. Then I went and got a book on the history of
baseball and mostly looked at the pictures. Old-time
ballplayers wore big, balloony uniforms back then,
and lots of them had droopy mustaches.

There are about a hundred million people who
think some general named Abner Doubleday invented
baseball. But it's probably not true. Nobody really
knows how baseball got started. There was a game
called Rounders that people in England played long
ago. It could have been the beginning of baseball.

But nobody really knows.

Nobody knows why people care about the game so
much either.

It's kind of dumb, when you think about it. A guy
stands on a little hill with a ball in his hand, the
pitcher. Until he throws the ball, nothing can happen.
Then some guy at home plate with a big stick in his
hands has to decide whether to swing at the ball or
not. If he hits it, everybody starts running around. If
he hits it really far, he runs around the bases until he
gets back to where he started.

He runs to first base, second base, third base, and
then home. Why do they call it *home* instead of fourth
base? Nobody knows.

Why do millions of people care about a silly game
like baseball? I don't know.

All I know is I have loved the game since I can
remember. I loved it because it was so beautiful to
watch. The green field and the red dirt. The way the
players move to catch and throw the ball.

I know I loved it because my dad loved it. I loved sitting next to him, watching games on TV, letting him explain to me everything that was happening. If my dad loved baseball, then I had to love baseball, because I wanted to be just like him.

And there's something else.

I loved the idea of the pitcher being in the middle of everything. In control. I always wanted to be that guy out there on the little hill with the ball in his hand. And if I didn't throw it, nothing could happen.

I got out my baseball book and read it from cover to cover. I looked at the baby stories I wrote that were so dumb. I looked at all the stuff I wrote about Bobby Baseball.

I really want to be famous. I know that. And maybe I want it too much.

It's my dream. To be a famous pitcher and make the Hall of Fame and then write books about baseball and me.

Now it looked like it was only going to be a dream.

I got two telephone calls that night. The first was from Jase.

"You quit? Is that right, what Sammy said?"

"Yep."

"But why? It's so dumb."

"I have my reasons," I said.

"Did your dad give you a hard time, or what?"

"That's part of it," I said. "If I don't pitch, I don't play."

"Well, unquit, or whatever. I want you back on the team."

"I'll talk to you tomorrow."

I went back to my room and did my homework.

But my mind really wasn't on it. Then I heard Mom call from downstairs, "Bobby? Another call for you."

I went into my parents' room to take it. To my surprise, it was Mouth.

"What's all this guff about you quitting? Is it true?"

"Yes," I said.

"Well," said Mouth, "it's the most unheard-of thing I ever heard of. And very dumb. We need you for the Rangers game. Come on back."

"You don't need me," I said. "Freddie can pitch."

"I know that, nerdo," she said. "But what about you? How can you leave your whole team in the lurch? How can I laugh my head off about something as stupid as Bobby Baseball if you're not around?"

"Thanks for calling, Mouth," I said.

"Don't be a quitter," she said. "Winners never quit, and quitters never win, don't you know that?"

"Who made that dumb saying up?" I asked her. "I have my own reasons for quitting. Personal reasons."

"Sheesh! I'm really disappointed in you, Mister Bobby Baseball. I didn't think you were the kind of guy to let his teammates down."

"Good luck on Saturday," I said.

"Hawks rule!" she said. "No problem."

Then we hung up.

It was a hard week to get through.

Jase and the other Hawks in my school kept after me, telling me to come back. I liked hearing it, but I wouldn't change my mind. On Thursday Dad and Sammy just went off to practice without asking me to come. I was talking to Dad again. Sort of. But we didn't talk about the team or my playing again or anything really important.

I tried not to think about the team. Next year I'd pitch for somebody else, I told myself, and even as I tried to fool myself, I knew it wasn't true.

Dreams die hard.

I slept late on Saturday, had breakfast, and hung out in my room. My team was going to play a big ball game today without me, and I felt funny about it. Sammy came into my room and asked if I was coming.

I told him no.

"You're making a mistake, Sneezer," he said, then left.

Grandpa was in the den downstairs, watching the "Game of the Week" on TV. I went down and sat there with him. The game was Pirates versus Phillies, two teams I didn't care about.

I looked at the game but I didn't see it, really. I kept looking at my watch. And my mind was on the Hawks.

Now Freddie was walking down the line to warm up, I was thinking. Now the Hawks were taking infield practice. Two o'clock came. Game time.

Now the Hawks were taking the field. I could see it all so clear in my head. Jase was on first base, warming up the infield. Mouth was out at second, talking a blue streak. Tony was chanting at shortstop. Dad was standing near the bench, clapping his hands. Sammy was writing in his scorebook. All the subs were yelling, "Hawks rule!"

I couldn't sit in the den anymore. I got up and walked outside.

It was a beautiful day for a ball game. Sunny, but

not too hot. In my head I saw Freddie rubbing up the ball, getting ready to make his first pitch.

I felt sad. I was all alone, and my team was far away. They were about to play, and I wasn't even there.

I couldn't stand not knowing what was happening. I felt helpless and stupid. I knew I wanted to be with my team. Even if I couldn't play.

I walked to the garage. I had to find out how the Hawks were doing. I had to be there, had to see the game, had to cheer on the Hawks and be part of them.

That's when I got out my bicycle and rolled it down the driveway to the street. Without telling anyone, I began to pedal across town to Schenley Park.

25

Spectator Sport

I knew I shouldn't be doing it.

I was breaking the rules. I wasn't supposed to be riding my bike across busy streets. I was supposed to tell my mom when I was going someplace.

Right then I didn't care.

I kept pedaling along, trying to be careful and still hurrying to get there. I stopped at red traffic lights and waited. I stayed way to the right and kept watch when cars went by. It was scary going through streets with lots of traffic.

It's a long way to Schenley Park when you're on a bicycle and not in a car. It took more than a half hour for me to get there.

But then I was in the park. I took the bike path and cut across until I could see the diamond where the Hawks and Rangers were playing. It was only then that I figured out that I didn't want Dad to see me. So I circled around the long way and came up to the ball field in back of the stands behind the infield. Then I walked my bike to a place where two sets of bleachers met and peeked out onto the field from there.

The Hawks were at bat. I looked up to a kid who was sitting in the bleachers above me and asked him what inning it was and the score. "Rangers ahead four–one, bottom of the third."

Mike Marder got on with a walk, and Mouth was coming up. "Let's go, Hawks!" I yelled.

The kid looked down at me. "The Hawks stink," he said.

"Sez you."

Mouth looked like a peanut in front of the big Rangers catcher and the umpire. The Ranger pitcher was big, too, and he was throwing hard.

Then Mouth bunted, a beauty, and scooted down to first before they could even pick up the ball. Our bench started yelling, and I did too.

"Way to go, Mouth!"

I could see Dad down behind third base, clapping for Mouth.

"How many out?" I asked the kid.

"Two."

It was up to Tony, who stepped into the batter's box and pushed his batting helmet down hard on his head, like he always does. "Tony!" I yelled.

"No batter!" the kid yelled.

Tony took a few pitches, then hit a slow roller the Rangers turned into a force play at second.

"What'd I tell you?" the kid said to me.

"It ain't over till it's over," I said.

I stood there holding my bike, fidgeting from one foot to the other, feeling that losing lump down deep in my throat.

"How'd the Rangers get four?" I asked the kid.

"Errors," he said. "The pitcher walked a couple, then the third baseman let one through his legs, the first baseman threw the ball away. Like that."

Mike had messed up, and so had Jason.

I started to feel really bad right then. And ashamed of myself. I should have been there, in uniform and on the field, even if I was only going to sit on the bench. I should have been clapping and cheering for my teammates. I should have been there to tell Jason, "Okay, get 'em next time." You're supposed to pick up a teammate when he makes an error or strikes out. You're not supposed to be watching the game from the stands.

Freddie was terrific in the top of the fourth inning. He struck out two. Jimmy's glove kept popping as Freddie blew it by the Rangers. He struck out two more in the fifth, but the Hawks weren't hitting at all.

I hated being so far away from the bench. I wanted to be out on the field, not hiding from my dad.

I walked my bike around to the Hawks' side of the field and locked it up on a fence. Then I climbed up the back of the bleachers and hoisted myself into a spot in the last row.

Freddie was untouchable in the top of the sixth. Ned was catching now, and he never had to get out of his crouch behind the plate. Strike, strike, ball, strike three! The next batter took two strikes, then gave a weak swing while trying to back out of the box. Two down.

Freddie was a real pitcher now, not some kid who could just throw hard. He knew what he was doing on the mound, you could see it in his eyes, in the way he moved, how he stood looking down at the batter just before he threw.

That's when I knew the dream in my heart was over. I only dreamed I was a great pitcher. Freddie really was.

"Freddie!" I yelled as he popped a third strike past the next Ranger batter. Then I was on my feet applauding.

Down on the bench I saw Dad turn his head. He looked up in the stands, and our eyes met and held for a second. I gave him a little wave with my hand. Then Dad turned away.

I was in deep trouble now, but I didn't care. All of a sudden a whole lot of other things were more important to me.

I wanted the Hawks to win the game.

I wanted to see a rally get started.

I wanted Tony to get a hit, and Gardy, and Ned, and Jackie, and Nan, who couldn't hit at all.

I wanted the subs to turn it around. But mostly I wanted to be on the field myself.

What was I doing up here in the stands? Stands were for spectators. I was a player. Maybe not a great one, maybe not even a very good one. But I was a player. My place was on the field or even on the bench, not up here in the stands.

I stood up and started working my way down the bleachers, walking and hopping between people. When I got down to the second row, I jumped and landed on the grass between the stands and the low fence that ran around the field.

The Hawks were coming up to bat. Dad was out coaching third. I stood near the fence right behind our bench. Then someone yelled, "Down in front," and I crouched down on my knees behind the fence.

"Let's go, Hawks!" I yelled, and Mouth turned around.

"Bobby Baseball!" she said in her loud voice, and half the kids on the bench turned around. Even Sammy, who stopped looking into his scorebook for once.

Sammy jumped up and came over to the fence. "Couldn't stay away, huh?" he said.

"Nope."

"Dad is gonna ground you forever," he said.

"I don't care."

Sammy looked at the swing gate that let players come on the field. "You're not in uniform," he said. "The rules say you can't come on the field."

"Please," I said.

Through his eyeglasses, I saw Sammy's eyes gleam. "What the heck," he said, "you could be a coach, right?" Then he opened the gate, and I scooted on the field and ran over to the bench.

"Let's go, Hawks!" I said. Mouth gave me a friendly punch on the arm, and Nan gave me a kiss, which I didn't want.

"Hawks rule!" Mouth yelled, and I joined her, clapping my hands. Everyone joined in: "Hawks rule! Hawks rule!"

It felt so good to be on the bench.

Ned Robbins stepped up to the plate with Tuck on deck.

"Ned-die, Ned-die!" we started yelling.

Ned swung and hit a line shot to the gap in left that rolled clear to the fence. It was a sight to see Ned run, his arms swinging, feet moving, belly shaking with every step. He huffed and puffed into second base before the Rangers could get the ball back to the infield.

Jase was doing his stork dance in front of the bench, singing away and yelling, "Kalarooty!"

Tuck stepped into the batter's box, and Jackie Ulman went on deck. Tuck took pitches and didn't swing and worked out a walk.

Two on, none out.

Right then I knew we'd win it. We'd come from behind right there in the bottom of the sixth, score a bunch of runs, and hold the Rangers in the seventh.

Jackie Ulman took a big swing and just barely topped the ball. It rolled down the third-base line, just in fair territory. The Ranger third baseman came running in, scooped it in his bare hand, and threw it—*wild* —down the right-field line.

Here was Neddie running like a turtle, Tuck right on his heels, the both of them coming across the plate while Jackie ran all the way to second base.

Four to three, Rangers; tying run on second; nobody out.

Gardy was coming up next, then Nan. Behind them the top of the batting order: KP, Tony, and Mike.

It was over for the Rangers. No way we wouldn't win it now. A couple more hits or walks or errors and we'd win it.

26

Wet Grounds

That's the way it would be in the movies or on TV. The underdog comes from behind at the end and beats the big, bad team. You see it a million times. But that's the movies, not real life.

We lost.

Gardy struck out, and so did Nan. She looked bad at the plate, like she always did, waving at a pitch she couldn't reach if she stood on a stepladder.

Tony rolled out to the shortstop, and the rally was over.

Freddie held the Rangers in the seventh, but the Hawks couldn't do a thing.

Final score: Rangers, 4—Hawks, 3.

The Rangers were better than we were. Just a little, but they were better.

The Hawks went out on the field to shake hands

with the Rangers. I stayed behind on the bench, with Sammy.

Then Dad came off the field. "Sit right where you are," he said to me. He walked over to Jack Sheridan, and the two of them talked a few moments, then shook hands.

The Hawks and Rangers players were going through the gate now, meeting family and friends and going home. Dad and Sammy picked up the equipment and packed it.

Then Dad came over. "Stay here, Sammy," he said. "I want to have a talk with your brother." He motioned to me with one finger, and I followed him out onto the diamond.

The stands were empty now, and so was the field. Out near the mound Dad stopped walking and turned to me. "Start talking," he said. "And you'd better make it good."

I looked up into Dad's hard face. For a second I didn't know where to start. I felt tears beginning right behind my eyes, but I wiped them away. "I apologize," I said, "for everything."

"How'd you get here?"

"On my bike. I know, that was wrong, too. But I couldn't stay home. I had to be here with the team. I was wrong to quit. I'm a Hawk. . . . I have to be on the team, win or lose . . . even if I have to sit on the bench . . ."

"You didn't say that a week ago," Dad said.

"I was wrong," I said. "I was stupid." Now my throat got really tight and tears began. I couldn't hold them back. "Oh, Dad, I wanted to be the best pitcher.

I had a dream . . . and I was going to make it come true. But I stink . . . I'll never be as good as Freddie."

Dad took out his hankie and handed it to me. I wiped my eyes.

"You have to let me back on the team," I said. "I'll even sit on the bench, I don't care. But I love baseball. I want to be around it or in it or anything you say. But please, Dad, let me come back." Now I was sobbing and I couldn't even speak.

That's when Dad moved close and put his big arms around me. He hugged me to him, and we rocked for a moment in the middle of the diamond.

"I was fooling myself," I said when my voice came back. "I thought I was so great."

"I know, I know," Dad said.

"But all I am is a weak-armed sub infielder who can't even hit."

"Like father, like son," said Dad. "Kind of runs in the family, doesn't it?" He squatted down to look in my eyes. "Listen, Bobby," he said, "the worst thing in the world is to find out you're not as good as you think you are. I know what you're feeling."

"But you were great," I sobbed.

"At your age? The best. I was a star, Bob-o. Everybody said I had a one-way ticket to the majors. And I believed it, too. Then the Cardinals signed me, I went off to Little Rock, and all of a sudden I found out I wasn't such hot stuff. Every day I saw players better than I'd ever be . . . guys who could hit 'em far and hit 'em often. I couldn't. Simple as that. That's when my dream died, when I was twenty years old."

"It hurts so bad," I said.

"Sure does," said Dad, "but it's better to find out

now than when you're twenty. You're just a kid. You'll have other dreams. I know how ambitious you are and I wouldn't ever bet you won't be exactly what you want to be."

I hugged Dad then and buried my face in his big chest. "I wanted to make you so proud of me," I said.

"I *am* proud of you," he said. "I am very proud that you're my son."

"Even if I stink?"

"You don't stink, Bob-o, you're as good as you can be. Which is good enough for me. Anytime and any-place."

I blew my nose in Dad's hankie. I just couldn't stop crying.

"Look at you," he said, "you're getting the field all soaked." He kissed my cheek. "There'll be wet grounds here tomorrow."

"Game called on account of tears," I said.

"I do love you a lot," Dad said. "You are a very great kid."

"Not lately," I said. "But from here on in."

●   ●   ●

The Death of Bobby Baseball
by Robert E. Ellis

**Once there was this kid who thought he
was the greatest pitcher in the world.**

Then he found out he wasn't.

**This kid gave everyone a hard time. He
was so sure he was going to be a superstar.**

Bobby Baseball is dead. I am not going to write any more stupid things in this stupid book.

I know I am not going to the big leagues or the Hall of Fame.

So this is good-bye, Bobby Baseball. The last thing I will do with this book is put it away in the back of my closet, where I won't see it for a few years.

Maybe when I am twenty, I will get this book down and read it. I will probably laugh my head off.

27

Postgame Summary

Dad made me sit on the bench for three whole games.
But I went to every practice and every game and did
every single thing I was supposed to.

I was a Hawk again, and that was enough.

There was even one more hard thing I had to swallow. Mouth was a better second baseman than me.
And she was a girl. But Mouth was my friend by then.
We got to like each other a lot. She kept teasing me by
calling me Bobby Baseball, but it was a fun kind of
teasing. Mouth got at least one bunt hit a game for the
rest of the season. And she never shut up about it.

The Hawks didn't win the championship. We
ended up with a win-loss record of 6 and 4. We lost to
the Bankers again and also to the Rangers.

And then, in the play-offs, we were eliminated by
the Lions, of all teams. They'd gotten a lot better as

the season went along, and we'd stayed about the same.

Freddie pitched great for us all season. But Dad was right about one thing: We Hawks never did hit well enough.

Jason didn't hit a home run, although he kept trying. And I got a couple of hits before the season ended. Even our hard-hearted official scorer, Sammy, gave me credit for poking two grounders through the infield.

I ended up with two hits in twenty-four times at bat, for a season batting average of .083. That's no way to get to Cooperstown.

At the end of the season, when the Lions knocked us out of the play-offs, Dad arranged a Hawks team party. He took us to Burger Baby, out near the bypass. We marched in fifteen strong, wearing our uniforms, and just about took over the place. It was great.

Neddie Robbins ate five hamburgers. If I hadn't seen it with my own eyes, I wouldn't have believed it. Nobody called Ned Jelly Belly anymore. He was a good player and he tried hard, even though he was so fat he couldn't move well. Neddie was very sad at the party. He told Mouth and me that he was going to a special summer camp, a diet camp called Camp Lean-Too, and he was sure he was going to hate it. "You'll do great," Mouth told him, and we both promised to write Ned over the summer.

The summer vacation was okay. Mouth and Nan showed up at Jason's house a few times, and we played basketball in his driveway. Jimmy Rossillo and Mike Marder came over to my house on their bikes, and we usually played Stratomatic Baseball.

In August my family went to the lake for two weeks. We stayed in the cabin we always rent.

At night, after dinner, we'd all sit on the big front porch and watch the water and talk.

I'd put my baseball book away by then, but I still had the feeling that I wanted to write stories. So when we went into town one day, I bought myself a new composition book and began to write some things in it.

About Grandpa's crazy made-up stories.

About Sammy the computer-head.

About Jase the ace, who danced every day and never worried about anything.

Jase was right about me. Lack of looseness is something I really do have way too much of. I'm trying to work on it.

But this one night on the porch I felt a new dream beginning to come clear to me. I remember how we were sitting around on our rocking chairs, with the moon making a silver path on the water of the lake.

"If someone was a really great writer," I asked Mom, "and wrote some really great books . . . could he get in the Hall of Fame?"

"A Hall of Fame for writers?" Mom said. "I don't think there is such a thing."

"They give prizes to writers, though," said Grandpa. "I know that."

"Really?" I said. "There are prizes for writers?"

"Lots of them," Mom said.

"Like what?" I asked.

"Well," Mom said, "there are the National Book Awards each year. For fiction, nonfiction, and poetry.

They're important. And I guess the Pulitzer Prize is pretty big, too."

"How about the mystery writers," said Grandpa. "Don't they give the Edgar Allan Poe Awards every year?"

"That they do," said Mom.

"There's probably a hatful of prizes we don't even know about," Grandpa said.

"What's the very biggest prize a writer can win?" I asked.

"Got to be the Nobel Prize," Grandpa said. "That's the biggie."

"They don't give that every year, though," said Mom. "But if a writer keeps going and writes lots of good books through a whole career, I guess the very biggest honor going is the Nobel Prize for Literature."

"Lots of Americans have won it," Grandpa said. "Sinclair Lewis and Pearl Buck, that Hemingway fella."

"More," said Mom. "William Faulkner, Saul Bellow, I. B. Singer . . ."

"Wow," I said. "That's terrific to know. Thanks a lot, you guys."

Off in the dark in the corner of the porch I heard Sammy begin to laugh. "There he goes again," he said. "Bobby 'Bookman' and his dreams of glory."

"Lay off, Sammy," I said, but he wasn't really far from wrong. My brother knows me pretty well.

First I figure I'll aim for a National Book Award . . . then maybe a Pulitzer, if I spelled it right.

The Nobel Prize I'll probably have to wait a while for.

Robert Kimmel Smith is a baseball fanatic. "As a kid I had two ambitions. One was to pitch for the Brooklyn Dodgers, the other to write books." He is the author of *Chocolate Fever, Jelly Belly, The War with Grandpa,* and *Mostly Michael.*

Mr. Smith follows the fortunes of the N.Y. Mets from his home in Brooklyn, where he lives with his wife, Claire. They have two children, Roger and Heidi, who are as baseball crazy as their parents.